MW01067837

ENEMY

AT THE

HELM

A NOVEL

MARK DICKSON

RIVER GROVE
BOOKS

Published by River Grove Books
Austin, TX
www.rivergrovebooks.com

Distributed by River Grove Books

Design and composition by Greenleaf Book Group
Cover design by Greenleaf Book Group
Cover photos by Vidar Nordli-Mathisen and Tomas Lundahl on Unsplash.com

Publisher's Cataloging-in-Publication data is available.

Print ISBN: 978-1-63299-731-9

eBook ISBN: 978-1-63299-732-6

First Edition

PROLOGUE

"YES! WAY TO GO!" TOM SAID to his student, who had just completed a proper sentence in English. He gave him a high five in pantomime on the computer screen.

Tom Jensen was a lanky twenty-three-year-old Texan with an easy smile who, after finishing college last year, wasn't ready to "adult" yet. His parents couldn't understand why he didn't try to get a "real" job with benefits and vacation time. His consistent reply was that all his friends with those real jobs were miserable in their cubicles. He knew his ADHD needed constant external stimulation and was not about to join his friends in their misery.

He was fortunate enough to travel with his family quite a bit over the years, and he enjoyed it so much that he decided he wanted to make a living doing that. He majored in international business in college and learned Spanish but didn't want to work for a big company. Instead, he wanted to live and work abroad. The only problem was that many Latin American countries forbade the hiring of foreigners. Their unemployment rate was so high that they wanted to save any available jobs for their citizens. In fact, they actually spent a relatively large percentage of their law enforcement budgets trying to ferret out the illegal employment of foreigners by businesses large and small.

Tom learned that the cost of living in Central and South America was very low if he stayed in youth hostels and lived like a local, so that was his first stop after graduation. He found a whole network of people who volunteered to work at hostels and small hotels in exchange for room and board. In that way, he could save even more money than he would otherwise have to spend on lodging and food. But he still needed to earn cash.

"You need to have multiple income streams," he remembered his dad telling him regularly. "You never know when something outside of your control is going to cut one off."

So he found his way to a school in Central America that taught people how to teach English to non–English speakers. Many program graduates got into classrooms in other countries, but even that was too confining for Tom because it required signing a contract for at least a year. He wanted the freedom to go whenever and wherever his interest took him.

He found out that there are companies that pair up students in foreign countries that will pay for individual English lessons. With a reliable internet connection, he could be anywhere in the world and teach students anywhere else, and the company would transfer his pay directly into his bank account. There were no insurance or retirement benefits, but the income was definitely enough to support himself in a developing country.

So he taught English to kids from halfway across the world for a few hours a day, used the rest of his time at his volunteer job, and explored his surrounding areas. He found that although he went into teaching as a means to an end, he actually enjoyed interacting with the students. He was a kid at heart and had no trouble motivating the kids to learn and return for more lessons.

He liked using props during his lessons to break up the monotony of conjugating verbs and changing prepositions. He would draw silly pictures on his whiteboard and use toys with funny voices to get his points across. On occasion, he would even give voice to his stray kitten that he would bring in front of the computer to engage the student.

During his volunteering, he met a lot of people who were also trying to make a living while traveling. They all had different ways of earning money, which fascinated him. One spent so much time surfing that he became good enough that others sought him out to teach them. Another wrote travel guides. Others sold things on the internet. One couple had a drone that they used to video small hotels and resorts to provide content for marketing in exchange for lodging. The drone was controlled through a device remarkably similar to the video game controllers he grew up playing with.

Like most young men his age, he was good at video games and decided he could produce the same type of video, so he bought a drone. He learned how to use it better after he crashed it into his first tree.

One day while teaching his student who took the English name Brian, he was having trouble keeping him engaged in the lesson. He started his drone behind him and brought it up to the camera so Brian could see it. It held a video camera and had lights that flashed in different patterns. That got Brian's attention, especially when he saw the kitten in the basket hanging from the drone.

The students always had their families around when they were taking their lessons. Brian was no exception, and they noticed when he was suddenly redirected back to the computer screen. Brian's father looked to see what was so enthralling—and smiled.

———

Eleven months later, Tom was now in Colombia, working on his multiple income streams. He had made his way to the small town of Necoclí, on the eastern shore of the Gulf of Urabá, between Panama and Colombia. The town was big enough to have good internet access, so he could keep teaching on his schedule. He also had several hostels and small hotels where he sold his video marketing materials using his drone. He also recognized that wealthy Colombians had large mansions along the shore and up into the hills that were unoccupied most of the year.

He convinced a few of the owners he met to allow him to rent out their mansions for short periods. He, in turn, marketed these to college students in the United States looking for an adventurous spring break. The owners got income, the students paid Tom to organize trips they could brag about to their friends back home, and Tom got to surf and hike the surrounding countryside when he wasn't working. He could easily make enough money to meet his expenses and save some for a rainy day. Everyone was happy.

One afternoon, he was enjoying a beer at a small restaurant over-looking the beach and called his dad to share his wonderful life.

"Well, hey, Tom, you caught me at a good time. I just finished a case, and I'm on my way to clinic, late as usual. What's up?"

"Hey, Dad, I just wanted to call and tell you how fantastic life is here. I've been taking your advice on developing multiple income streams, and it's paying off! Nothing is happening right now, so I'm taking a break, hav-ing a beer overlooking the beautiful Caribbean from here in Colombia."

John Jensen quickly did the mental calculation, "It's two in the after-noon there, and it's Tuesday." He could feel his blood pressure rising already. He was a surgeon who considered anything less than a fifty-hour workweek a slow week. He needed to work that hard to pay all his office and personal expenses and build up his retirement fund.

"I'm glad you're enjoying life, son." *If he's enjoying life, he's not being productive*, thought John, who knew plenty of people who "enjoyed" every penny they made with no thought toward planning for a rainy day. "Are you putting anything aside for savings?"

"Yeah, a little."

A little, John thought as he felt his face redden. "You know, you need at least six months of living expenses saved up as an emergency fund." *Before you start enjoying life* went unsaid.

"I know, and it will take me a while to get there, but everything is more relaxed here. I like it. Plus, I can get by on very little income. There's a lot of bartering going on here."

"That's fine, and good for you for keeping your expenses low. I just know you're a smart kid and a hard worker. People naturally like you. You could start your own business here and do great, then sell your com-pany in several years and live high on the hog forever after that. Or start another company and do it over again. You can do so much better."

Here we go again, thought Tom. *He just doesn't get it.*

"Here's a proposition for you," John said. "Quit your little adven-ture now. Time's a-wastin'. If you want to get started with an established company, they'll be less interested if they see you spent the last several years bouncing around Latin America. I'll help you get home and talk to some people who can help you get started. It's time to grow up now.

I really think it will be better for you, and you'll be happier in the long run."

Ugh. "Thanks for the offer, Dad, but I'm gonna stick around here some more. I'll be fine, I promise."

"All right, but if you change your mind, let me know. I know your mother would like you back here soon also."

Not fair, thought Tom. *Time to end this now.*

"All right, love you, and tell Mom I love her too."

"I love you too. Be careful," John said as he hung up. *When will I ever get through his thick skull?*

There were two men at the table next to Tom, speaking Spanish. One said to the other, "April 15 will be the Día del Puerto, bzzzzz." They smiled and clinked their glasses in a toast.

Tom thought that was strange. Who talks like that? And why the buzzing sound at the end? His Spanish was good, but maybe he didn't understand a local idiom, or maybe it was a holiday he didn't know about. He finished his beer, paid the small tab, and returned to surf some more.

ONE

"C'MON, DAD, LET'S GO!" Billy Haggard yelled to his father, Chuck, as he grabbed his hand to pull him along the passageway from the check-in area to the ramp leading to the cruise ship.

Chuck looked at his wife, Theresa, while wrangling his suitcase and backpack. "Go ahead—I've got the other three."

Billy was the youngest of the Haggard kids at eight years of age. His parents had first brought up the idea of a Caribbean cruise to the children about two years earlier, and Billy had watched every TV show and YouTube video he could find about cruises ever since. Now, on April 15, it was finally happening. He was beyond excited and couldn't get to the ship fast enough.

Theresa smiled and looked at his brother and two sisters, the oldest of whom was sixteen. They were excited also, but too cool to show it like their baby brother. At least they were old enough to help their mother with the luggage and bags. They got through the luggage drop-off, and then Billy took off again down the path marked by the arrows. They all met up at the embarkation photo station and found Billy trying on the pirate hat, jumping up and down, and yelling at the rest of them to hurry up.

Once the photos were done and the family made their way to the gangway, Chuck stopped them, saying, "Remember, everyone, the buddy system. No one go anywhere alone. Your mother and I can't be everywhere at once, so I'm going to need all of you to look out for each other, okay?"

Chuck had been worried about the safety of the kids since he began hearing stories of predators taking advantage of young people on cruises. He learned that there was no governing legal authority on these ships when they were at sea, and these monsters would get away with crimes ranging from sexual assault to sometimes even murder.

Chuck was a broad but fit man of Irish heritage with a steely glare that could pierce even the hardest opponent. He had spent the last fifteen years at the New York City Police Department, the previous ten in their Human Trafficking section of the Vice Enforcement Division, where he rose to head the Internet section. As part of this, he spent a lot of time on the dark web, hacking into groups of people who tried very hard to hide their illicit activities. He saw some truly horrifying things on a regular basis and couldn't help but forbid his kids to do a lot of seemingly harmless things that many of their friends were able to do, like go to the mall without a parent.

He thought about different ways to keep up with the kids, from two-way radios for everyone to mandating that no one be without him or Theresa, who finally told him he was being unreasonable. "They'll be fine," she said. "They're good kids, they'll look out for each other when they aren't with us, and besides, they make good decisions."

"They're teenagers, for God's sake!" Chuck replied. "Have you ever known a teenager to make a good decision?"

"I promise you—they'll be fine. We'll get the family suite, so we all have to be in the same room, and we can have breakfast delivered for us in the mornings. Plus, we know the kids' areas on the ship where they will be spending most of the time. We can make the rounds frequently. They'll be fine, I promise."

He finally decided that she knew the kids better than he did, and then they spent the next two years saving up for that family suite on the aft of the ship with the big balcony. Two days before they left for Miami, he sat everyone down and read them the riot act. "I know you guys all have good heads on your shoulders and wouldn't intentionally do anything you shouldn't. But there can still be bad guys on board who are very good at taking advantage of people without their knowing it. The best way to deal with that is to never be alone. So I want everyone to always be with at least one other family member, never without another family member. It's called the buddy system. Got it?"

"Yes, Dad," they replied, almost in unison. He thought that was weird. He expected protest. *Maybe Theresa already talked to them about this*, he thought.

The day finally arrived, and Billy raced up the gangway to the final shipborne security station. Once they all got through and the crew member told them how to get to their room, the kids looked at each other and yelled, "Scatter!"

And they all went in different directions.

Chuck stood there open-mouthed and slowly turned his head to his wife. "I thought you said they were good kids!"

"Relax, they'll be fine." She patted his arm. "Come on, let's go find the room."

His blood pressure started rising—he could feel it.

One by one, the kids came back to the suite, and together they attended the lifeboat drill. The crew members came by with complimentary drinks for everyone, and after the training, Chuck said to his wife, "That helped. Let's go find a bar."

"Aye, aye, Captain," she replied. "You go ahead, I'm going to stop in the ladies' room, and I'll meet you there. Get me something good!"

They kissed, and she went inside to find the restroom. He gave his best dad's glare to the kids. "Remember, buddy system." They rolled their eyes as they nodded affirmatively. He looked out on the ship's port side as they glided past other vessels and buildings lining the channel they were sailing down. He noticed the Coast Guard vessel matching their speed along the ship's port side and felt better. *That's a good sign*, he thought. *There really are other people working hard to keep us safe. Maybe this will be okay after all.* He continued to walk forward along the port side outer deck with the kids, enjoying the warm breeze on his face.

———

The captain of the giant cruise ship, *Leviathan*, with eight thousand passengers and three thousand crew members, was ready to leave the dock at PortMiami for its weeklong cruise. He looked over at the ever-present US Coast Guard escort, awaiting final clearance to depart. The ship had finished loading the last of its 1.2 million gallons of diesel fuel just an hour earlier.

"*Leviathan, Leviathan, Leviathan* . . . You are clear to depart," radioed the Vessel Traffic Service (VTS) on Marine VHF channel 14. Jointly operated by the United States Coast Guard, the VTS monitors all the surrounding waters with radar and shipborne assets. Any large ship is a target at any time, but a cruise ship with eleven thousand people on it, going slow in a small channel, was a giant, ripe, low-hanging fruit just begging to be picked.

The Coast Guard cutters are the larger seagoing vessels that most people think of, but they are too big and unwieldy to defend against a small, nimble boat that can be only twenty feet long but can carry thousands of pounds of explosives. So the Coast Guard uses smaller boats with a crew of three that can be considered similar to a border collie herding a flock of sheep. These Defender-class boats look like a bigger version of a zodiac inflatable boat, but with a small cabin housing a commander and a driver, and armed with a 50-caliber machine gun at the open bow, staffed at all times by a coastguardsman in constant radio contact with their commander. These boats can exceed fifty miles per hour on open water, making them ideal for intercepting any perceived threat on the water.

With the radar from the Coast Guard station tracking waterborne vessels and radar from the nearby airports and defense installations tracking airborne ones, combined with the multiple eyes of people on Coast Guard vessels in the area, those in charge felt confident that they could detect a threat in enough time to either convince it to change course or disable or destroy it well before it could do any damage.

Until today.

The officers of the *Leviathan* had spotters on the bridge and both sides of the ship, fore and aft, looking out for hazards that could set a bad and ominous tone for the rest of the cruise—in many cases, the type of vacation families have saved for years to be able to afford. A great many of these vacationers were looking out at the surrounding waters and boats and buildings from their perches on the decks or from their cabins. Some were watching the Defender maintain its speed in tandem with the lumbering cruise ship on its right flank.

No one saw the small drone approach the twenty-five-foot Defender from the rear, only a foot or two above the water. Even though the drones typically make a fair amount of noise, no one on the Coast Guard boat could hear it over the sound of the engines, especially with their headphones in place. The drone had no trouble exceeding the slow forward speed of the boats, rising up and over the cabin until it was in position. It thus was not seen by the crew until it dropped to head height two feet in front of the front window.

"What th—" said the commander.

The people on the ship's port side were struck by a large flash and boom from the Defender. The gunner never had a chance, taking the full brunt of the two-and-a-half pounds of C4 plastic explosive. The commander and driver were shredded by the shards of windshield safety glass that also couldn't withstand the impact. The boat was instantly out of commission.

Which meant the *Leviathan* was defenseless.

"Captain, this is port side spotter. There has been an explosion on the Defender, and they are dead in the water."

The captain instantly declared, "Issue a Mayday call and slow down to stay even with the ship. Deploy lifeboat twelve to help recover any survivors."

The comms officer called, "Mayday, Mayday, Mayday. Coast Guard Station Miami, this is *Leviathan*. The Defender on our port side is on fire—there appears to have been an explosion. We are deploying a lifeboat to assist survivors."

The Coast Guard station was on an artificial island near the mouth of the Government Cut, which was just a canal and the exit point for all the major ocean-going vessels going into and out of PortMiami. This included cargo ships, cruise ships, and thousands of fishing and personal boats. It is only five hundred feet wide and almost fifty feet deep, leaving plenty of clearance from the keel of even the largest ocean-going ship.

Since there were always small boats in the area, several diverted toward the fireball. One, a deep-sea fishing boat with twin outboard motors, had been chartered the previous day by Ian Ndobo, a second-generation Briton with parents from Nigeria.

Ian had been recently released from a British prison after serving five years for assaulting a police officer intervening in Ian's alcohol-fueled aggressive courtship of a young lady that quickly turned physical. In other words, he was abducting her. While in prison, he had been befriended and protected by a group of Africans who convinced him that his parents weren't escaping terrorism as they told him as a boy. Rather, they had given up on their people and went to live as traitorous capitalists, taking advantage of their people instead.

He was so enraged by all the injustices his fellow prisoners told him were imposed on his kinfolk by the capitalists that he was an easy target for their associates once he was released. These associates took him in and provided him with hot food, clothing, shelter, and further indoctrination until they deemed him ready for the next phase. They sent him to South Florida to make a new life two years ago and helped him get a job as a travel agent. Since he spoke with a British accent, the Floridians thought of him as an expert in all things foreign.

He did very well and was able to buy a small house on one of the canals off the Intracoastal Canal that had a dock, although he had no boat. He also could easily afford the luxury of a deep-sea fishing expedition for himself the day before. He had killed the captain while out at sea, dumped his body, and brought the boat back to the dock at his house.

Under the cover of night, he took ten pounds of shaped charge C4 that his friends' associates had given him and, using industrial marine tape, secured it to the bow of the fishing boat. This would ensure that the explosive power would be focused on one point to penetrate multiple layers of steel. He then loaded the cabin of the boat with boxes holding one hundred pounds of magnesium and another hundred pounds of a mixture of rust and aluminum powder.

On the afternoon of April 15, he filled the tank and slowly made his way to the Government Cut. Since the authorities were used to seeing this boat make this trip daily, they thought nothing of it. When the Defender exploded, all attention was devoted to it. Surrounding vessels immediately changed course to assist, including Ian, who opened the throttle.

As he neared the stricken Defender, he didn't slow but changed course to head directly for the site of the internal fuel tanks of the *Leviathan*. The shaped charge of military-grade high explosive delivered to the cruise ship's hull at forty miles an hour acted like an armor-piercing tank sabot round. The explosion destroyed everything in front of the fishing boat for fifty feet, including the double hulls of the *Leviathan*. It came to stop in the same compartment as the fuel tanks. The magnesium did the rest. When mixed with water, burning magnesium becomes a blindingly white, superhot ball of energy that melts everything nearby. It cannot be extinguished.

Furthermore, the magnesium ignited the rust and aluminum powder mixture, known as Thermite. At three thousand degrees, this quickly melted the fuel tanks. The hydrogen gas produced by the magnesium and thermite exposed to the salty seawater added to the explosive power, resulting in a violent explosion that rocked the entire ship before it settled into a list to the port side.

The cruise ship captain and bridge crew immediately began their emergency procedure for the disaster when the second drone flew into the bridge from the open starboard door. When this drone detonated its cargo of C4, there were no more senior officers on the ship able to direct the rest of the crew to lifesaving and firefighting efforts.

The *Leviathan* drifted obliquely into the channel before sinking rapidly onto its left side. Those healthy people exposed on the upper decks and balconies were in the best position to swim to the nearest boat or shore. Approximately 5,000 other vacationers and cruise ship staff weren't so lucky.

The loss of life and property was bad enough, but the real damage was the wreck's location. Since the ship was over 1,100 feet long and the Government Cut was only 500 feet wide when the ship sank obliquely across the cut, it blocked the passage of other large ships.

PortMiami, the tenth-largest port in the United States, was now closed for business.

At the same hour, similar size vessels, including cruise ships and freighters, were also being sunk in the other nineteen largest ports in the country, all sinking in such a way as to block the usage of the ports for all trade and commerce. It was the single worst day in the history of the US Coast Guard.

—

The liquid petroleum gas (LPG) tanker Teekay *Fremont Spirit*, flying under the flag of Singapore and captained by Lars Jorgenson, had just entered the Miraflores Locks of the Panama Canal. His ship was built to barely fit into these locks that carried 40 percent of the shipping business between Atlantic and Pacific Ocean countries. The other 60 percent had previously gone around the southern tip of the coast of South America in larger ships. The government of Panama, which received many thousands of dollars in transit fees for each ship that went through the canal that had been built by the United States over one hundred years ago, realized it could get even more fees if it could accommodate these larger vessels, so they commissioned and built a newer, larger canal alongside the original one. Now 60 percent of boat traffic came through the new Panama Canal, which doubled the tiny country's revenue.

It was completed at a good time because the Chinese had recognized they were vulnerable if the time ever came when they could no longer send their massive volume of exports through Panama. They had convinced the neighboring country of Nicaragua, both financially and otherwise, to let them build a new canal through that country, and they were nearing the completion of construction. Not only were they about to be free of the threat of reducing their trade, but they were also going to profit even more from other countries' trade that didn't even involve them, much like the Americans profited for decades before they handed over their golden goose to the Panamanians.

Captain Ricardo Montoya was at the helm of his very large crude carrier (also known as a VLCC), the *Exxon Explorer*, bringing crude oil from one of its offshore fields in Indonesia to Houston via the new Panama Canal. He glanced over at the *Fremont Spirit* below him on the right. He did not see the drone packed with C4 drop down the smokestack. However, one of the spectators on the viewing platform of the canal did, and he asked his wife, "Did you see that?" He pointed to the ship, and his wife turned to look.

Captain Montoya then saw a small explosion involving the *Fremont Spirit*'s midportion. The spectators on the viewing platform saw it, too, and were mesmerized. Captain Jorgenson heard and felt the explosion, trying to learn what happened. In fact, the drone had exploded close enough to the engine room to set the fuel tanks ablaze. More importantly, it damaged the cooling pumps that kept the propane mixture liquefied at −120 degrees Fahrenheit. After a few minutes, the blaze was hot enough to melt through the containment vessels for the liquid natural gas, which turned to vapor as the temperature rose. As the gas vaporized, it became more flammable.

The resulting explosion completely obliterated any solid object within five hundred yards, including the spectators on the viewing platform and the locks on either side of the ship. The resulting rush of water out of Lake Gatun overwhelmed the other downstream lock, and it then failed as well. There was no way to hold back the water, which was now a torrent destroying everything in its path to the Pacific Ocean. The huge Lake Gatun was being emptied, and there was nothing anyone could do about it.

Captain Montoya had been blinded by shattering glass when the secondary explosion erupted, and he didn't see the three drones that targeted his ship. One hit the bridge where he was located at the same time that another hit the rudder area on the stern of the vessel and the third also went down the smokestack. When that drone exploded in the fuel tank area, it didn't cause a secondary explosion, but it melted the containment vessels of the crude oil, causing it to spill into the surrounding lock. Two million barrels or eighty-four million gallons of crude oil were now filling the lock occupied by the stricken carrier.

The operators of the new canal now had two huge problems: a VLCC stuck in a lock because it had no power or steerage and a looming environmental catastrophe if those two million barrels of crude were allowed to escape into the Pacific Ocean. It would make the Exxon Valdez disaster in Alaska look like the aftermath of a fraternity party. They realized they could not open the locks. The ships en route in both directions would be grounded once Lake Gatun was emptied. The Panama Canal was now closed for business for the next several months at least. The Panamanian government would have to figure out how to do without the more than $150 million per month it received from the canal, or 28 percent of its annual revenue.

———

Captain Abdul al-Mohammed was piloting the Suezmax LPG carrier *Ishtar* flagged out of Iraq, taking its product to the refinery in Marseilles, which would convert its energy into fuel for Europeans. He didn't care, and most people didn't know, that the great French engineer Eiffel, builder of the iconic tower in Paris, had visited the Suez Canal. He also didn't know that Eiffel had tried to replicate the canal feat in Panama by cutting a long sea-level canal from the Atlantic to the Pacific. It was after his backers finally ran out of money that the Americans took over and devised a different way to skin the cat in Panama. The Suez Canal had recently been enlarged, and now one out of every eight products traded on the planet went through it.

Captain al-Mohammed was approaching another LPG carrier traveling in the opposite direction through the canal when he saw a flash of light to his right. As he turned his head to identify the source, his ship was struck by a powerful and loud jolt. He was never able to see the Yemeni who fired the shoulder-mounted RPG because another one from his port side fired another RPG into the bridge, killing everyone inside. It was essentially a point-blank shot because the canal was only about 650 feet wide. The perpetrators reloaded and fired two more RPGs into the holding tanks of the carrier, where the natural gas again vaporized and produced a massive secondary explosion. This explosion was so big that it ignited the approaching LPG carrier as well. Both ships were now dead in the water, and the Suez Canal was closed.

In one day, world trade came to a screeching halt.

TWO

"YOU'RE FIRED," THE US PRESIDENT SAID to Admiral Charles Gardner, commandant of the Coast Guard, during the emergency meeting of the National Security Council (NSC).

"Yes sir," the admiral replied, gathering his papers. He then stood, saluted, and wheeled around to leave the Situation Room—his thirty-year career abruptly ended.

"Who can tell me what the hell happened today?" asked the president as the door closed behind the commandant.

The remaining members of the NSC looked surreptitiously at each other, trying to determine who would next absorb the wrath. Finally, the national security advisor, Norman Singletary, spoke up. "Sir, it appears that we have sustained a coordinated attack on our largest twenty ports in the country. At least twenty large ships have been sunk in the main approach channels of these ports. Some were cruise ships, some were large cargo ships, and at least two were crude oil tankers. In addition, the Panama and Suez Canals had similar disasters."

"Who did it, Norm?"

"Well, sir, we don't know yet. This only happened within the last four hours. Rescue operations are still underway."

"Right, rescue," he said almost as an afterthought. "How many people have been killed?"

"It's too early to have any firm numbers yet, but we know tens of thousands of people on these ships were affected."

The president paled. This was potentially worse than September 11,

2001, an event and response for which he'd criticized the then-sitting president mercilessly. He held that leader responsible so he could score political points, and he knew there would be many opponents of both parties looking to do the same to him.

"How did it happen?" he asked.

The Department of Homeland Security secretary, Danielle Haverford, replied, "What we know now is that just prior to the large ships being attacked, there was a small Coast Guard vessel nearby that seemed to spontaneously explode."

"Spontaneously?"

"We're still trying to figure out how that happened. But the response protocol to that is for every able-bodied vessel nearby to drop every-thing and get to the injured boat as quickly as possible. There seemed to be one boat in each of these cases that sped toward the injured vessel but then veered off late and hit the target. In addition, there are reports that the senior officers on all the ships were taken out, but we don't know how."

The president was getting exasperated. "What do you mean you don't know how?"

Secretary Haverford explained, "In some cases, people nearby saw small flashes in the vicinity of the bridge of the large ships after they experienced their catastrophic damage. We have been unable to find any senior officers alive, so we think they were secondarily targeted to pre-vent a good response to the disaster. This may have been a simple way to magnify the damage."

"Well, how are you going to find out? Was this an inside job? Were there RPGs or something? Who is in charge of this?" He was starting to lose his composure thinking of the looming political disaster.

The chairman of the Joint Chiefs of Staff, General James Corrigan, spoke up: "You just fired him, sir."

The president reddened. "All right, then, you take charge."

"With all due respect, sir, the US Coast Guard has jurisdiction over all territorial waters. They have the personnel, infrastructure, technol-ogy, and relationships with all the relevant people and agencies to sort through this most effectively."

Anthony Grimes, who had been on the job as attorney general for a total of two weeks after his predecessor was summarily dismissed, said, "Mr. President, in other terrorist actions against the United States, the FBI has taken the lead in the investigation. May I suggest we take that route?"

"Good idea," replied the president. "Get the director in here and bring him up to speed."

Grimes answered, "We don't have a director yet. You still haven't nominated anyone to that position."

The president liked to micromanage as much as possible and didn't think that was a problem usually. But this was becoming a multifaceted problem that exceeded his ability to oversee everything.

"Okay," he said, trying to focus his response to the crisis. "Danielle, since you're DHS and this happened on the homeland, you take the lead for now. You have authority to ask anyone in any department to give you what you need to get to the bottom of this."

"Yes, sir," Haverford replied, wondering who in the governmental bureaucracy she could ask for such help. She had spent her entire life outside of the public sphere and only just recently realized that the Coast Guard was a part of DHS. And now her commandant was history.

"Let's adjourn for tonight and have a full Cabinet meeting daily, starting tomorrow at 9:00 a.m.," said the president, tiring of the lack of definite answers so far. "I want not only an update of progress so far but also an assessment of what the effects are going to be going forward." Even though he liked to micromanage many things that prior presidents delegated, he still was able to grasp the big picture and understood that effects could be widespread.

THREE

THE DEPUTY DIRECTOR OF THE FBI, Frank Burroughs, was a thirty-year veteran of the Bureau, rising from a rookie to an assistant special agent in charge, or ASAC, in Pittsburgh when one of the airplanes hijacked on September 11, Flight 93, crashed near Shanksville, Pennsylvania. He'd been in charge of the gathering and analyzing the millions of pieces of evidence at that site. He realized the value of methodical, tedious, and decidedly unglamorous running down of even the most mundane of leads.

At the same time the president was meeting with the NSC in the Situation Room in Washington, DC, Burroughs was on a conference call with the special agents in charge (SACs) in all twenty of the cities affected by the port shutdowns. He knew that the scope of the disaster was enormous for any individual port, but nationally it was potentially catastrophic.

"Ladies and Gentlemen, I don't need to remind you how epic the implications of this attack may be," said Burroughs. "We need everyone on deck, turning over every leaf, interviewing everyone breathing near these ports. Mobilize your people tonight. These crime scenes are going to be massive."

The SACs deployed people to every aircraft and marine radar site, Harbormaster office, Coast Guard station, police and sheriff and Border Patrol office, looking for anything unusual that could focus their hunt for the perpetrators. One of those people was Special Agent Sam Jensen, out of the Seattle Field Office.

Sam was still a fresh-faced thirty-two-year-old agent who had only been in the Bureau for five years. Six-foot-two, with close-cropped blond hair, and regular time in the gym, he epitomized the stereotypical FBI agent. He had the confident air of a man ready for just about anything. He had been assigned to the Seattle Field Office fresh out of the Academy in Quantico, Virginia, and loved his life in the Pacific Northwest.

This was the biggest case of Sam's career, even though he was tasked with, as he called it, "looking under rocks." His older brother John was very proud of him and was envious of all the "cool things" that he thought FBI agents did. He wouldn't have been so envious if he had realized just how many rocks had to be looked under.

Sam, on the other hand, thought his big brother was the coolest person ever. John was a surgeon in Texas, and Sam got to watch him work in the operating room a few times when he was younger. He was impressed by his calm, confident way of approaching life-threatening problems and regularly defeating them.

This mutual admiration resulted in lots of phone calls back and forth, and today was no different. While other agents were sent to the various aircraft and marine radar towers, Sam was dispatched to find and interview as many individuals as possible in the region of their crime scene, which was the mouth of Puget Sound. Once a strategic point, this area had since been reconfigured into three state parks—Fort Worden, Fort Casey, and Fort Flagler State Historical Parks.

That this area was a crime scene was no accident. The mouth of Puget Sound was fairly narrow and only about two hundred feet deep. Large ships easily exceed this height, so when sunk, they significantly obstruct navigation.

He started with Fort Casey State Park because it was the least difficult to reach from Seattle. At 0700, he drove off the ferry, turned left, and was almost immediately at the parking area, already overflowing with people of all shapes and sizes looking out at the bustling activity in the water, hoping to catch a glimpse of the wreckage.

It was going to be a very long day.

After parking illegally on the grass, he retrieved his notebook and made his way to the beach, where hundreds of people were lining the shore to watch the activity between the Puget Sound and the San Juan de Fuca Strait. There were dozens of official-looking boats in the water between Fort Casey and Fort Worden State Parks. There were also a growing number of cargo ships and tankers appearing in the San Juan de Fuca Strait to the north. Because they hadn't yet figured out the exact location of the sunken ship in relation to the underwater topography and the vastness of the potential crime scene, no other boats or ships were allowed near the area.

Sam started at the south end of the crowd, pulled out his notebook and pen, and methodically recorded their names and contact information and their recollection of what they saw and heard if they'd been there the day before. It was mind-numbing work, but he forced himself to stay focused, aware that the smallest detail could help piece together the big picture.

Several hours later, as he made his way through the crowd northward, his phone rang. Looking down, he saw it was his brother, John, no doubt wanting to know what he found so far. He still had a lot of people to interview and didn't want anyone to leave while he was doing something else, so he let it go to voice mail and continued his plodding through the crowd. *I need to just keep going like John does during his long operations*, he thought. *Quitting is not an option.*

Most of the people weren't present yesterday. But a few were, and they gave their stories in varying detail. As dusk was closing in, he got to the northern edge of the crowd at the Admiralty Head Lighthouse. One young couple on bikes with GoPro video cameras on their helmets had stopped for a picnic near the line of trees overlooking the inlet the day before, and Sam questioned them.

"I thought it was odd when we saw one dude standing by a tree by himself," said Austin, the grungy hippie-looking one. "After the explosion, he looked like he put something away in his backpack and then left. Everyone else was trying to get closer to the water to see better, and he went the other way."

Sam was writing furiously, thinking he may have discovered something important. "Can you describe him?"

Sarah, his tattooed girlfriend, said, "We can do better. Our helmets were sitting on the picnic bench, but we forgot to turn them off. The batteries were dead by the time we got home, but after recharging and watching them, we realized the guy was there."

Now Sam was getting the tingly feeling he always got when closing in. "Where is that video now?"

"Right here," said Austin, taking his helmet off and showing Sam the video camera.

"Did you make a copy?" asked Sam.

"No," said Sarah.

"How can I look at them?"

"We'll just show you," said Austin.

They retreated from the sunlight and watched the footage on the two-inch screen together. Sure enough, they saw what appeared to be a man about fifty feet away standing next to a tree holding something. They heard the explosion, and the man watched a few more seconds before putting the object in his pack and walking to the right, out of camera view. It looked to Sam like he might have been Asian, but that was a stretch given his distance from the camera and the tiny size of the screen.

Sam knew this was important. "Can I take this?" he asked. He knew he could subpoena it, but this was much faster.

"Of course," said Sarah. "Whoever did this just killed tons of fish, maybe an Orca or two. You guys need to find him and string him up, then filet him alive!" Sam was always amazed at how quickly the peace, love, and harmony crowd could turn vicious.

"Thank you, ma'am. We'll do everything we can to do just that."

On the ferry back to Seattle, he called ahead to his chief at the field office to make sure the science and technology whizzes would be ready to examine the videos. He paused, exhausted, and then he remembered that John had called earlier. He listened to the voice mail: "Hey little brother, I know you're busy, but believe it or not, I may have something helpful for you."

Sam groaned inwardly to himself. He loved his big brother, but he was the type who knew a little bit about a lot of things. While his breadth of knowledge impressed a lot of people, when he encountered a professional in that field, that person tended just to nod politely. Sam did that a lot with John.

Sam spent the rest of the ferry ride back to Seattle typing his report on his laptop. He immediately took the camera to the tech whizzes. He stood by as they first made copies of the videos and then manipulated—enlarged and enhanced—the images as much as possible.

The technicians made notes about everything they could identify, and when they came to the frames that showed the object the man was carrying, they paid particular attention. "That looks like a video game controller," said one. "Why would a guy go to Land's End and play video games by himself?"

The other tech replied, "You know, that looks a lot like my drone controller."

Maybe this was a worthless chase, thought Sam. Maybe the guy was just another nerd out playing with electronics by himself.

———

The same process was ongoing at every affected port. Agent Paul O'Malley was assigned to interview everyone in the bars along the waterfront at the Port of New York and New Jersey, hoping to find someone who might have seen something. He was at the Angry Dog, sitting at the bar nursing an O'Doul's, when he overheard a guy three stools down say, "My buddy in the 415 said they had it coming."

O'Malley had heard of the 415. They were a moderately large group that protested in New York, Boston, and Washington, DC, every April 15, which happened to be the day everyone in the United States was required to file their tax returns *and* pay their taxes. Members of the 415 thought the income tax system was unconstitutional. Since many people were intrinsically distrustful of anything government-related, O'Malley knew he shouldn't identify himself as an FBI agent. Instead, he played the sympathetic bystander. "Good for them. It looks like all the things they've been talking about finally resulted in somebody acting on it."

"Somebody acting on it? My buddy said that they were the ones who did it!"

O'Malley now had an awful lot more work to do to get to the bottom of this. He spent the next few hours at the bar talking to and commiserating with his new targets, getting to know more about where they worked, what they did there, where they lived, what their family lives were like. After they peeled off, he got more information about them from the bartender and then left and went to his special agent in charge with his info and a request to set up a sting operation. His SAC knew this would be a complex and prolonged process involving multiple agents and a significant amount of his budget. He would have to get approval from his higher-ups to pursue this. A slip by any of them at any time could endanger the entire effort to find the perpetrators.

———

FBI Special Agent Stefano Alvarez from the Miami Field Office was assigned the unenviable task of trying to identify the provenance of the deep-sea fishing vessel that slammed into the *Leviathan*. If there was anything left, the remains of the boat and its occupants lay underneath the sunken giant cruise ship.

The first destination for Agent Alvarez was the Harbormaster's office on Dodge Island, directly across the channel from downtown Miami. The Vessel Tracking Service (VTS) was there, and he wanted to see what they had learned about the day of the attack and, hopefully, the few days beforehand. He was directed to the chief of the department, Victor Tremayne, who led him into the small room that housed the monitors displaying maps and schedules of current, departing, and incoming vessels.

"We're getting our information on locations of these vessels through the AIS, or Automatic Identification System. The ships have transponders that continually broadcast their locations and speeds to land-based stations, other ships nearby, and even some satellites."

"Like aircraft transponders?" asked Alvarez.

"Essentially, yes," replied Tremayne.

"So you can go back in time and see a track of the ship's movements?"

"Up to a point."

"What do you mean?"

"First of all, there's a time limit on the data we keep. We only keep the last two weeks' worth of data. That's not a problem in this case because we knew exactly when and where the incident occurred, and we saved that info right away."

"Great," answered Alvarez. "Let's see it."

"It's not that simple, I'm afraid."

Alvarez was getting a bad feeling in the pit of his stomach now. "Let me guess, the bad guy found a way to turn off his transponder."

"You FBI guys really are quick learners! It's actually easier than you might think. The Iranians do it a lot with their tankers as a way to try to evade sanctions placed on their oil exports."

"Are you saying the Iranians did this?"

"Maybe, maybe not. I can't say they didn't do it, but they could have. But lots of other people can turn off transponders too. The military, for instance, routinely turns theirs off when they are on missions that require a stealthy footprint. It's not rocket science."

"Okay, so if the transponder is off, would there be other surveillance radar or photo or video evidence of what happened?"

"Maybe," replied Tremayne. "The Coast Guard may have radar data. And we have a webcam, but this happened just outside the range of the camera. You can only see the bow of the cruise ship that got attacked."

"All right, let's look at that anyway. Maybe we can see something useful. Load up that video stream for me while I call the Coast Guard to start the radar ball rolling."

FOUR

THE ENTIRE CABINET ATTENDED the daily NSC meeting in DC for the first major update on the investigation and assessment of the effects of the attacks two days before.

"What have we got now?" asked the president.

DHS Secretary Haverford took the lead. "As of 0800 this morning, sir, we've identified that twenty ports in United States waters have been attacked in one form or another, and the Suez Canal and both of the Panama Canals are destroyed enough to be out of commission."

She had been extremely busy over the last forty-two hours or so. The Department of Homeland Security encompassed not only the US Coast Guard but also US Immigration and Customs Enforcement, US Customs and Border Protection, the Transportation Security Administration, the US Secret Service, the Federal Emergency Management Agency, US Citizenship and Immigration Services, and the Cybersecurity and Infrastructure Security Agency. All of them were working continuously to get a handle on the damage and try to find the perpetrators. When she considered that none of her responsible departments were able to get any warning of this, she was surprised that she still had her job.

"Vice Admiral Chester Green, the chief of the Eastern Division of the Coast Guard, is acting commandant. He says we've lost seventeen Defender-class boats with fifty-one coastguardsmen on board, at least twenty-three large ships, including twelve cruise ships, nine large freighters, and two LPG tankers. Rescue operations are still underway, but we have been able to confirm now that at least thirty thousand people have been killed. We expect that number to rise."

"Defense?" asked the president.

Secretary of Defense David Donaldson answered, "Sir, we have been monitoring defense posturing of all the world's armed forces, and not one of them has changed since the attacks. Furthermore, since we didn't see any of these attacks coming, we were concerned that enemy submarines might have been responsible. But none of our subs or sonar installations around the CONUS found anything out of the ordinary." He was referencing the standard acronym for the Continental United States. "In addition, we didn't see any airborne assets such as airplanes or missiles that could have hit the ships."

That there was no military evidence was itself telling. No state actor could accomplish an event of this magnitude without leaving some trail.

"State?" The president was settling into the groove now. Like all other politicians, he was a narcissist, although he hid it less well than the others. But he was also a successful businessman who was able to run any meeting to get the most useful information.

Secretary Aubrey Stallings III replied, "Mr. President, we have been in contact with all the major nations and half of the minor ones, and all have expressed their condolences and offered their assistance if needed."

"Any whispers behind the scenes, Aubrey?"

"No, sir. Usually, there is some finger-pointing under the table, but we aren't seeing that yet."

"Fine," said the president. "Justice?"

Attorney General Grimes said, "Sir, the FBI has agents all over the country beating every bush to try to get some answers. The only things we have so far that may be helpful are one guy in a bar in New York Harbor who said the domestic protest group 415 did it, one guy in a merchant marine bar in New Orleans who overheard someone else say it's going to be a lot quieter there from now on, and a guy in Puget Sound who may have been flying a drone and then left without it. Also, the Miami attack vessel had its transponder off. We're checking to see if that is the case at the other locations, also. If so, that implies a little more forethought by these perpetrators to try to avoid identification, as opposed to the classic Middle Eastern groups that we tend to think of first in these kinds of terrorist attacks."

"What does that mean?" asked the president. "Any ideas?"

"We try to look for patterns that we can use to narrow our focus going forward in cases like this where there are multiple seemingly related events," said Grimes. "The common factors that we have so far are that large ships were sunk in the channels that access the twenty major ports of the United States, as well as the choke points of the major trade routes of the world, the Suez and Panama Canals. And then there's the port in Houston. Many of these in the US had Coast Guard escorts, which were taken out prior to the ships being sunk. The large ships were sunk after being rammed by smaller vessels of various types already in the area. In every case, these big ships are blocking access to the ports. There is no radar evidence of attack by air, but radar can only detect objects greater than a certain size. We have two reports so far that may indicate something smaller might have been used. Drones are smaller, and they can carry small payloads. Plastic explosives come in small packages."

Grimes went on, "We don't know this is what happened. But we are going to look closer for evidence that supports or disproves this."

"Okay, good," said the president. "So, are these ports completely blocked?"

"Yes, sir," replied DHS Secretary Haverford.

"How long until they are cleared and back in service?"

"Our best estimate is that this will take several months at least, maybe longer," Haverford said. "And not only that, but once the channels are back open, every ship owner is going to want to be sure that his property is going to be protected. We are going to have to fix our security of the ports. And that is going to take an unknown longer length of time."

"Well," said the president. "We've been needing to get back to making more things in America again anyway, so maybe this might be sort of a good thing."

The commerce secretary, Stephen Chambers, spoke up: "Mr. President, there is more."

"Yes?"

"These US ports carry ninety-eight percent of the import and export traffic of the United States. Sixty percent of the cargo that goes through the Panama Canal begins or ends in a US port. If these are blocked for months, it would lead to such a disruption in trade that it would lead to a massive economic slowdown. It would make the Great Depression look like the go-go nineties. And this will affect the rest of the world, not only because we are a huge producer and consumer of a big percentage of total world output but also because the Panama and Suez Canals account for about twenty percent of world trade. The economic engine of the planet has just seized up."

"But we've got a lot more airports than seaports," said the Transportation secretary, Frederick Timmons. "Why can't we use them like we did during the Berlin Airlift?"

"First of all," said Chambers, "we were supplying a tiny number of people with basic necessities in Berlin. Even then, it took around-the-clock flights landing a fully loaded cargo aircraft every sixty seconds for weeks to keep those people alive. It was an incredible hardship for the population of West Berlin, who would have starved to death if the Soviets hadn't given up their siege."

"Second," he continued, "there is a great deal of products traded between countries that are too bulky or heavy for aircraft. They simply can't fit."

"Third." He was rolling now. "The proportion of the economy devoted to international trade is huge. Well over two trillion dollars' worth of goods come through US ports every year, both imported and exported. That's a lot of stuff. And it takes people to make that happen. Over twenty percent of the jobs in the US—more than forty-one million people—are supported by international trade. Can you imagine an unemployment rate of over twenty percent? It will likely be higher than that because of follow-on effects."

That got everyone's attention. The attacks were a big problem, to be sure, but now this was looking like a long-term catastrophe. "This is a real economy-killer, Mr. President."

"Shit," said the president, who grasped the implication instantly. "Find these bastards."

FIVE

THE SPECIAL AGENT IN CHARGE of the Seattle Field Office, Stan Clarkson, was briefing the fifty agents under his command. "I just got off a conference call with the deputy director, who has been compiling all the factors involving these harbor attacks." He summarized the data collected so far. "A big puzzle has been why the Coast Guard Defender boats all exploded. Thanks in part to Special Agent Sam Jensen of this field office, there is reason to believe that airborne drones may have been involved. They are too small for radar or the casual observer to notice, and boat engines can mask the noise that they make. Plus, they can easily carry a couple of pounds of anything, and a couple of pounds of high explosive, such as C4, can do a lot of damage to a small area.

"I need the following five agents to start focusing on the possibilities of this, the evidence we have so far, and the possible relations to all the known and unknown drone owners and operators in the region." He named the agents, which included Sam Jensen. After the briefing, the five agents met quickly with the SAC to coordinate their efforts—then Sam walked to his car. On the way, he remembered his brother's voice mail and called him back.

"Hey, John, sorry it took so long. What's up?"

John replied, "No worries, man, I know you've got your hands full. I just had some information that may or may not be helpful to you. You know my son Tom is in Colombia right now, right?"

"I knew he was somewhere . . ." said Sam, who was wondering where this was going.

"Well, he is currently at a small seaside town using his drone for video marketing for hostels and hotels and whatnot, and he called me after the harbor attacks and said that about a month ago, he overheard a couple of guys talking at a restaurant there."

Sam was getting impatient now, but he forced himself to listen more.

"He heard them say April 15 was going to be the Día del Puerto, and then he heard them make a buzzing sound."

Sam remembered enough Spanish from high school to translate, "Day of the port?" Then, "Harbor Day?" He recalled the briefing he just left about drones possibly being used. "Give me Tom's number, please. I'd like to talk to him personally about this."

———

"Well, hey, Uncle Sam!" Tom said when he saw his uncle's caller ID on his phone. He loved saying that, even though Sam wasn't that much older than he was.

"Hey, nephew Tom," Sam said—his standard reply. "Your dad just told me about the conversation you overheard a month ago about April 15. I want to talk to you about that."

"Sure," said Tom. "It's probably nothing, but I thought it was weird."

"In what way?" asked Sam.

"Well, they said 'Día del Puerto,' but I didn't know of any such holiday or saint of that name. I thought maybe I am just not well-versed in the local vernacular."

"Okay," said Sam. "Then what?"

"Well, then they toasted each other and made a buzzing sound."

Sam agreed that was weird but asked, "Have you heard that sound elsewhere in your travels in South or Central America?"

"Not that I've noticed."

"Hmmm," said Sam as he got to the point. "Your dad told me you got a drone for Christmas. Are you using it?"

"Am I using it? Only about every other day now. It's been a great way to break the ice with business owners who love to see their properties from a different angle. It's been a big help getting new business."

"I only know a little bit about drones. Do they make a buzzing sound?" asked Sam.

"Yeah, kind of, I guess. I actually have mine right here. Do you want me to launch it but keep it close so you can hear it?"

"Yes, please."

Tom started it up and made it hover near the phone. "Can you hear that?"

It sounded like a buzz to Sam. "Yes, I can. Tell me, what is the range on those?"

"Oh, they can be controlled a mile or more away, easy."

Sam started to get the tingle again. "And can they carry anything more than a little camera?"

Tom laughed. "Sure they can. Amazon is using them to deliver products to people in certain cities. They can probably carry up to five pounds or more."

Sam thought he might be onto something. "So, have you seen these two guys since then?"

"Yeah, there's only a few restaurants on the water here, and everyone comes here. I've probably seen them five or six times since then."

Now Sam was getting excited. "Do you think you could find them if I came down there to help? I am an FBI agent, after all, and finding people is what we do."

"Absolutely," replied Tom. "If they are still in the area, it will be relatively easy if you have a few days. We will run across them, I'm sure." Tom was getting excited. None of his other family had been to visit him yet in his adventures, and his cool uncle was going to make a special trip.

"Let me see what I can do to convince my boss to send me," said Sam. "I should know something within a couple of days. In the meantime, try to quietly get some more info on these guys, like maybe where they stay or shop or work."

"I'd love to!" *This sounds like it may be another adventure*, thought Tom. *Can my life get any better?*

SIX

PAUL O'MALLEY WAS BACK in the bar talking with the guy whose buddy was in the 415. He was wearing a wire, and one of the buttons on his shirt was a tiny wireless video camera. He normally would have a handful of backup agents nearby, but because everyone was chasing mountains of leads, there was only one available, and he was a tech guy monitoring and tweaking the feeds. *Important*, admitted O'Malley to himself, *but I hope I don't need any muscle on this job.*

"So, has anybody heard if the IRS was affected by these attacks?" He left the question in the open for anyone to answer.

"I've got a cousin whose husband works in one of their call centers. He says they are sweating, big time," said a guy two stools down.

"How so?"

"Apparently, a lot of people file late in the day on April 15 to try to make the government wait as long as possible to get our money, but those are the same types of people that are glued to the TV when something major happens, so they missed their filings."

"Okay, so what? They just file a day or two later and pay the penalty."

"I thought so too," answered the man, "but the population isn't doing that. Those people are holding on to their cash. The IRS geeks are saying that forecasts of an economic depression are causing people to start hoarding cash. They are figuring the government will take months or years to come back to them to get it. By then, they may or may not have the money or a job to generate it. They're taking their chances with the money in their pocket now."

"Good," said O'Malley. "It was never the government's money any-way. They just take it from us under the threat of force, without caring what it does to us to have less as a result. Good to see them suffer too." O'Malley was playing a part in getting in good with the 415 crowd if possible, but he harbored the same basic emotions when it came to taxes. Except he knew that some of those taxes went to feed him and his family.

"You know, I've been looking for better ways to fight against these IRS guys. You think the 415 is a way to do that?"

"It may be," answered the man as he glanced toward the door. "But this guy here can answer for sure." He jerked his thumb toward a very large man walking in who looked like Paul Bunyan, right down to his plaid shirt and jeans. "Come have a seat. Jack Upshaw, meet Paul—"

"O'Leary," piped up Paul.

"So, Paul here thinks the same way we do and is looking to help with the cause," said the man.

"Well, we're always looking for help, aren't we," said Upshaw. "We're having a meeting tomorrow night if you want to come."

"As luck would have it, I don't have anything scheduled yet. Sure, I'll come. See if there's anything worthwhile I can do."

———

Agent Stefano Alvarez was tired from working eighteen-hour days. He got a copy of the webcam feed from PortMiami and was watching it on his home laptop for what seemed like the thousandth time, looking for some new evidence he hadn't seen yet. His method in times like this was to examine a tiny corner of the video screen several times to see if some-thing seemed out of the ordinary. He would record his notes on that, positive or negative, and then move to the adjacent tiny box of the video and repeat the process. It was laborious, but it meant that nothing got missed because everyone else always focused on the big event and didn't see minor details that might help crack the case.

He had already talked to the US Coast Guard station, whose radar was focused out to sea for incoming threats, so they were unhelpful. He had spoken to the people in the surrounding boats at the time of the incident, but no one could give any concrete information about the big fishing boat that had detoured into the cruise ship. They were all focused on the burning Coast Guard boat, understandably.

He was hoping against hope that the video would give him some thread of information he could start to unravel. He decided to give his burning eyes a break and went to the bathroom. Then he grabbed a beer from the fridge and plopped on the sofa, pinching his eyes shut. After a few minutes of refreshing his thirst and his eyes, he went back to his computer.

He picked up where he left off, which was now just to the starboard side of the cruise ship's bridge. He could only see the front third of the ship and the bridge. The explosion occurred on the inside of the bridge, so the eyes naturally gravitated toward that, but he was focused on the outside of that side of the bridge. Something bothered him, but he couldn't put a finger on it. He focused harder, and on the twelfth time viewing it, he was able to identify a transient abnormality in the building directly behind that area outside the bridge. In one frame, it was clear. In the next, it appeared a little blurred and then was clear again just before the explosion. He didn't know what it meant, but he made a note to tell the techies to do their thing on it tomorrow.

Since he was coming up dry in his efforts to identify the assaulting boat or its owner or driver, he would have to start calling every fishing boat operator in the area. He was not looking forward to that.

———

Necoclí, Colombia. Sam Jensen had easily gotten the approval from Clarkson, who detailed another agent, Joe Park, to follow up on the possible Asian drone operator at Puget Sound. He thought that if an Asian was involved, the most likely culprits would be from China or North Korea, and he knew the Chinese liked to use the North Koreans to do their dirty work.

Sam flew to Cartagena, rented a car, and met his nephew Tom at his apartment. Sam looked around the spartan place. It was studio style, with a hot plate in the kitchenette, a laptop on an overturned box in front of a sofa, and a couple of empty beer bottles in the sink. *Oh, to be young again*, he thought.

As they left the apartment, Tom explained, "Since I'd seen them at this one restaurant more than once, and I'm friends with this superhot waitress there, I thought she might know more about them."

"Good start," said Sam, thinking his young nephew might have a good head on his shoulders after all.

"She said they come to her place every Tuesday afternoon for lunch and stay through siesta. She doesn't know where they work, but they always seem to have plenty of money and always pay in cash."

It was Tuesday, so they were likely to see these men.

As they walked to the restaurant, Tom continued talking. "She said they sit at the same table outside on the deck every time, so I asked her to save a table for us next to them. They always speak Spanish, so I will sit closest to them with my back to them and translate quietly for you."

Wow, thought Sam. *He's really thought this through.*

When they arrived at the entrance to the restaurant, Tom waved hello to his waitress friend. "I can see why you like this place," said Sam. He had noticed that most of the women he had seen in Colombia so far were gorgeous, but this girl was off the charts. Maybe she was the reason the other two guys also liked to come here regularly. He heard her say something to his nephew as she led them to their table.

But when they got to their table, Sam saw that all the tables around them were empty. Tom leaned forward and said to Sam, "Linda said they should be here at the table behind me within a few minutes. Let's get a couple of beers and look at the menu."

As she brought the beers, the two other men arrived as if on cue. They caught Linda's eye, and she smiled and motioned her head toward their table. They sat down close to Sam and Tom, just as expected. She left and returned shortly with two beers for the new arrivals.

Sam studied the men as he and Tom ordered their meal. They were about thirty years old, and the taller one appeared fitter than the shorter one. Sam was good about figuring out when something was out of place, but he realized he was at a disadvantage because he didn't know the local customs and dress. So he couldn't tell if they were locals or outsiders.

Tom said quietly, "This ought to be good. This is what we have been working for." Sam realized he was translating now and looked elsewhere and nodded. He was looking toward the entrance when another man, about forty and heavier, walked in and headed straight for the men's table. He sat down, and Sam looked at Tom, raising his eyebrows in a question. Tom frowned a little because this was a new development and gave a slight shrug of his shoulders. *Okay,* thought Sam, *this is either a wrench in the works, or it's very important, or it means absolutely nothing.* He loved this part of police work, methodically investigating and eliminating the various possibilities until the question answered itself.

He noticed the new man pull an envelope out of a pocket and slide it across the table to the taller man, who smiled and placed it in his pocket. Tom translated the new man, "Your work in Houston was better than expected. The boss is very happy."

Sam instantly knew they needed more information. But how to get it? He had no jurisdiction here. He knew the Houston Ship Channel was the major location for the import and export of all things petroleum-based, and it had been knocked out of commission when a liquid natural gas tanker exploded at a terminal at its mouth. The resulting conflagration spread rapidly and destroyed most of the infrastructure supporting the tankers and refineries. The state of Texas was in serious trouble, not to mention the rest of the country.

"Thank you very much, my friend," said the taller man through Tom. "I hope we can do more business together in the future."

"I will pass along your gracious offer," the older man replied. "Now, what is good here?"

With that answer, Sam realized the new guy was not a local. Beyond that, he couldn't tell where he was from. He filed that away so he could ask Tom later if he could differentiate Spanish accents.

The two tables enjoyed their lunches, and by the time it came to pay, Sam had decided he needed to follow the men as long as possible. The two younger men seemed to have knowledge of the operational details of the attack, but Sam was confident the older man would lead to the decision-maker. He had Tom with him, who could help with local knowledge but might be a hindrance if it came to actual police work. He was sure the targets would split, and as they were settling their bills, he decided to follow the older man.

He motioned to Tom to stay put for a minute after the other table left. Then they, too, went out the front door onto the street. Sam looked left and then right, and his heart skipped a beat. All three men were about a block away, so Sam and Tom turned right to casually follow them. The men turned left, went two more blocks, and then turned right again. As Sam and Tom made the final right turn, they were face-to-face with the three targets.

"Why are you following us?" the taller man said in Spanish.

Tom answered quickly, "We are not. We are going back to my apartment."

"You look like police," the older man said to Sam. As Tom translated for Sam, the shorter man produced a knife out of nowhere and swung it at Tom in an underhand arc from his right side. Neither Sam nor Tom was expecting this, but Tom instantly reached down and out with the back of his wrist, catching the knife-wielder's wrist, and then reached over with his right hand to grab the man's elbow and violently rotated it toward him while pushing his wrist back. Sam heard a pop. The shorter man screamed and dropped the knife. He fell to the ground, clutching his arm.

Sam's eyes got huge, and he instinctively went to the ground to grab the knife so that none of the assailants could get it.

The taller man used that instant to come at Tom with his own knife, like a fencer going for the heart. Tom raised his left arm ninety degrees at the shoulder, stepped to the right, and grabbed the taller man's right wrist as it was coming for him but guided it under his left armpit. Tom pinned the man's wrist by dropping his arm, and as the man tried to pull his hand back with the knife, he found he was stuck. He tried pulling back harder just as Tom hit him under the chin, forcing his head back. Tom then hit him as hard as he could in the throat. The man's eyes widened. He moved his mouth without making a sound and then grabbed his throat with his free hand. Tom continued to pin the now-frantic man's knife arm, and after a minute, the man slumped to the ground and became still.

This happened so fast that after Sam grabbed the dropped knife, he looked up just in time to see the man grab his throat. While they watched him struggle to breathe, the older man ran down the street and turned at the first corner.

Together they turned to the seated man holding his arm, crying. They didn't know if it was because of the pain, seeing his buddy die, or losing the obvious payoff. It didn't matter. Sam had some zip ties in his pocket, and as he was putting them on the man, he said to Tom, "Holy shit, where on earth did you learn that?"

"Well, you know my dad. He always tries to be prepared, right? He researched crime in Latin America and found that knife attacks were the most common violent crime. So he taught me a couple of moves he learned in his Brazilian Jiu-Jitsu training. At the time, I thought, 'Okay, sure, Dad.' I never imagined actually having to use it."

John did Jiu-Jitsu? I thought his idea of being prepared was having a garden. Maybe having Tom around isn't going to be a hindrance at all.

"I think you dislocated his shoulder," said Sam. "He should be pretty compliant for us now. Tell him, please, that we are going to take him to get medical help." *He doesn't know that my idea of a doctor is the legal attaché at the nearest consulate.* "We need to get our things. We may be gone awhile." Together they went back to Tom's apartment and collected Sam's suitcase and Tom's backpack, where Tom threw in a couple of changes of clothes and his toiletries and, seeing his drone in the corner, tossed it in as well.

———

In Puget Sound, FBI agent Joe Park had been assigned to investigate retail stores that sold drones. With the Seattle area being so tech-heavy, that meant a lot of stores. He showed the picture from the GoPro camera to everyone behind the counters and left copies that they could show to their colleagues who might come in later. Late in the afternoon, he answered a call from one of the stores he had visited not far from the ferry terminal.

"Hi, I may have sold your guy a drone," said the voice on the other side of the connection.

Agent Park grabbed a pen and paper. "Tell me about it."

"It was about a month ago, and this Asian guy came in to buy one. He stood out to me for a few reasons."

"Go on," said Park.

"First, he had an extremely thick accent. I'm used to Asian accents, but this was hard even for me to understand."

Pretty weak, but okay, thought Park.

"Next, he came in with absolutely no knowledge of drones."

"Well, isn't that why people go to stores these days? To get educated on certain products?"

"Yeah, but this was different. Most people have a little bit of knowledge about a product and how they want to use it. But this guy not only had no clue about how to choose or operate a drone; he wanted it for an unusual reason."

Now we may be getting somewhere, thought Park.

"What was that reason?"

"He wanted it to carry something. I thought it was weird because, literally, everyone else wants to take pictures or videos with their drones. They think of carrying capacity in terms of how big a camera they can put on it. The only people up here who are focusing on carrying freight are the Amazon people. And they clearly have some tech knowledge that this guy didn't have. Not only that, the weirdest thing was the object he wanted to carry."

"And what was that?"

"I asked him how much weight he wanted it to carry, and he couldn't say. Maybe he didn't have enough English vocabulary. I don't know. But he finally said he wanted it to be able to carry a cat."

SEVEN

THERE WERE ABOUT TWENTY PEOPLE in the room, including two women, when Paul O'Malley showed up for the 415 meeting. It was a working-class neighborhood in Bayonne, New Jersey, where a great many of the residents were directly involved in the maritime trade. All the people there looked like they belonged in that neighborhood; none of them looked like hedge fund managers.

They greeted each other with animated familiarity—until they saw O'Malley. They then became more subdued, even wary. Finally, Jack Upshaw spoke up.

"Friends, I want to say how good it is to see all of you safe and sound. Of course, we are continuing to grieve over our friends that were lost and pray for their families and the quick recovery of the survivors. This series of events has affected all of us and will continue to do so for some time."

O'Malley couldn't tell if Upshaw was admitting they were involved or if they had friends and maybe family members who were on the affected ships.

"You know, it was bad that we had to have so many good people die, but ultimately what will happen is the government will get less of our money." O'Malley couldn't understand how that would happen, but he continued to listen, hoping to find out.

"These people who owned and used these vessels will no longer be paying taxes, and anything to decrease the government's cut is a good thing, right?"

Right, thought O'Malley. *You can't pay taxes when you're dead. This sure seems like a crazy way to get your point across.*

"But more importantly, all the other incidents across the country are multiplying this effect by the hundreds. We are finally going to starve this government into submission!"

O'Malley was well aware that there were now a few pairs of eyes on him. He tried to stay as cool as possible but realized he might be in the lion's den, with no real support if things got ugly.

———

The nearest US consulate in Colombia was in Barranquilla, an eight-hour drive from the Jensens' location. At least it was less than the fifteen hours it would take to get to Bogotá. Plus, there were always protests of some sort in the capital—best to avoid any complexities if possible. It was going to be an uncomfortable ride for their prisoner, but they couldn't risk air transport. Too many eyes would be on the three of them. *Oh, well. He shouldn't have destroyed the Houston Ship Channel.*

Sam called ahead for the legal attaché and gave him a heads-up. He also gave him a description of the older man and his last known location. Before they left Necoclí, they went back to the restaurant to ask Linda about him. She had never seen him before but thought his accent was from somewhere south. That didn't help much. Almost everything was somewhere south from there.

The attaché mobilized the discreet doctor they had on call for sensitive problems like this and contacted the local commander of the Policía Nacional. It was a risk, but Colombia was becoming more friendly to the United States after receiving billions of dollars of aid and matériel over the years. He next called the ambassador in Bogotá, who quickly arranged a flight to Barranquilla.

By the time Sam, Tom, and their prisoner drove through the compound's gates, the embassy officials were ready in a secure room deep inside the building. The man shrieked as his shoulder got popped back into its socket by the doctor, who turned and left the room without saying a word.

The interrogation went on for hours. Sam and Tom went to get some rest.

The next day the legal attaché updated the information to the deputy director of the FBI, Frank Burroughs, back in DC. The prisoner gave up what he knew, which wasn't much. He and his friend had been mid-level drug cartel members looking for work after the cessation of the drug war in Colombia. They were approached by a man they knew only as señor Rodriguez. They didn't know where he came from, but he had said his boss wanted to "pay back the Americans for what they did to his country." He had given them $100,000 and the task of destroying the Houston Ship Channel on April 15. On that day, their contact supplied them with a plan, a drone with a C4 payload, and intel on the ships in the channel.

———

There were plenty of Latin American countries that had issues with the United States and blamed the nation for their problems, but the one that made the most sense as the origin of the attack was Venezuela. Its petroleum industry had been collapsing ever since it was nationalized, and its leaders repeatedly blamed the United States for losing the associated income.

Burroughs, of course, was getting additional information from his other field offices as well and gave it to the National Security Council, which was meeting twice daily.

"Mr. President, we are gradually developing this case, but there is some conflicting information."

"Go on."

"In Colombia, we found people that were involved in the Houston Ship Channel attack." He explained the details he knew of so far. "From their investigation, they think the plans may have originated in Venezuela. However, our people in New York identified a group called 415, who perennially are involved with protests against the IRS that always occur on April 15 to call attention to what they claim are unjust taxation policies.

"Furthermore, we think the man with the controller that walked away from the Puget Sound inlet after the attack appears to be Asian.

We think we are closing in on him, but he is moving locations faster than we can keep up."

So, what's the conclusion, then?" asked the president.

"We have elements that suggest a common origin, Mr. President," said Danielle Haverford, the DHS secretary. "The targets were all sea-going vessels in major harbors. The perpetrators not only sank those vessels but blocked the harbors from being used for the next several months at least. In addition, the intel required to pull this off suggests a major operation has been underway for some time. Finally, the general method of attack, by eliminating rapid response by armed Coast Guard units, was well-thought-out beforehand and consistently executed on the same day at virtually the same time. And one more thing—one of our agents in Miami discovered that all of the boats that directly attacked the larger vessels had no active transponders."

The president asked, "Who could have the capabilities and the motive to do this?"

"It's pure speculation at this point, sir, but there are many potential adversaries that are currently enjoying our predicament. However, we have evidence of at least three different potential sources at this time. The Houston Ship Channel attacks seem to have been carried out by South Americans from Colombia, perhaps under the direction and with financing from someone in Venezuela. That would not be surprising, given the Venezuelan president's animosity toward the US—and you in particular."

"Yeah, yeah, yeah," replied the president with a flip of his hand. "What else?"

"The 415 group may be responsible for the attacks in the Port of New York/New Jersey. They have a long history of protesting against what they call oppression by the federal government through burdensome taxes. They have even called for a new American Revolution in the recent past. This could be a shot in that direction."

"And?" The president sensed there was more.

"Well, sir, if the Puget Sound terrorist was from Korea or China, there is no doubt that their leaders are antagonistic to the US, to say the least. Bottom line is, these three countries have a long-standing beef with us that they have talked about acting on recently. Plus, the Iranians love to turn off the transponders of their oil tankers to try to evade your new sanctions. We don't have any direct evidence of their involvement, but I wouldn't be surprised if we find some later. And there could be others that we haven't been able to track down yet."

"Well, dammit, why haven't you?"

"We are still in the early phases of investigating this, sir," answered Deputy Director Burroughs. "We are shaking all the trees around, but even one attack like this takes a while to get the answers. Twenty attacks just make it twenty times harder and will take longer as a result. I don't know how long it will take, but rest assured. We will track them down."

"Shake them harder, then!" exclaimed the president as he closed his briefing book, stood up, and strode out the door while his handlers struggled to keep up.

EIGHT

SIX DAYS AFTER THE ATTACK, Chuck Haggard was back
in his New York office overseeing the human trafficking section of the
NYPD. His wife, Theresa, had been in the ladies' room on *Leviathan*
when the massive explosion hit. The authorities still had not found her
and suggested to him that based on his description of her last known
location, it might be another two to three weeks before they could get to
her underwater area. He knew she was gone; he only hoped it had been
quick and painless for her. It wasn't painless for him or the kids, though.

When the Defender-class Coast Guard vessel exploded, all five
stopped and watched the scene. Chuck was as mesmerized as the other
thousand or so passengers and crew that were on that side of the ship.
Together they watched the nearby boats rush toward the stricken vessel and the crew members launching the lifeboat from their deck. Out
of the corner of his left eye, Chuck had seen the fishing boat change
direction and speed up until it crashed into *Leviathan*. The resulting
explosion was like nothing he had ever encountered before. When the
ship slammed back down on the water and immediately started listing to
the left, he heard the other explosion way above his level. All of a sudden, it was pandemonium, and it was all he could do to get eyes on his
four kids.

He knew something catastrophic had happened, and the likelihood
of an organized, methodical rescue effort was slim. He also knew they
were all good swimmers, and they weren't far from the edge of the channel. He told them to jump and swim as fast as they could, and he undid

a couple of life preserver rings and threw them in the water. Billy was scared and didn't want to jump, so Chuck picked him up by his collar and belt and threw him overboard, knowing the other kids would take care of him. He then turned to go back to get Theresa but could not get past the throng of humanity trampling over each other to get out of the interior of the ship. He held on to the nearest pole while standing on his tiptoes to see any sign of her as the boat continued to list more and more steeply.

From his training and general personality, he was pretty calm under extreme pressure, so he held his position as long as possible, hoping she got out without him seeing her or made it out a different exit. He kept telling himself this as the deck he was on tilted more and more, and the speed of the collapse accelerated. At the last minute, he jumped free and swam as fast as he could to the nearest shore.

He was reunited with his kids an hour later, and together the five of them huddled on the shore, staring silently at the ship, which was now completely on its left side. They were then ushered to a nearby location with other victims to be given aid, warm, dry clothing, and help with what to do next. There was also a section of law enforcement types who were taking statements from witnesses. Chuck naturally gravitated toward them, and after he identified himself as NYPD, he described what he saw. He knew it wasn't much, but he was hoping that some talented agent would be able to piece enough of the evidence together to figure out who had done this. And he *knew* it was an intentional attack.

His in-laws came down to Florida to help him with the kids and returned to New York after they had no sign of Theresa for three or four days. The in-laws were great about taking charge of all the kids, while Chuck stayed in touch with the investigators in Florida. He finally realized he wasn't helping by continually calling them, but he needed to do *something*. He then realized he had skills that might help the investigation. As the leader of a team of very talented men and women who were able to dive deep into the dark recesses of the internet to find truly evil people, he was a firm believer in the phrase, "The best defense against evil is good people skilled at violence." So he went back to work.

———

Joe Park had driven straight to the store in Seattle where the sales kid had called him from. He was surprised to see that the clerk was Asian, too, as he hadn't detected an accent during their phone call.

"So, is this the guy you sold the drone to?" He slid the GoPro picture across to him.

"It's too far away to see his face clearly, of course, but he looks to be the same height and build as the guy. And his hair color is the same," he said laughingly. "But the other reason I think it's him is the controller."

"What do you mean?"

"Look at the shape. Every manufacturer has a different controller. Different dimensions, antennas, joysticks, buttons—colors even. This particular controller is only made by one manufacturer, and it's the same one I sold him."

Park was feeling better about this now. He got the info on the exact make and model of the drone and immediately called his superiors to see if other locations had seen the same drone.

"How did he pay for it?" Joe asked.

"That was the other thing," the kid replied. "He paid in cash, but he had trouble counting it out. I had to help him get the right denominations."

"And you said he had a very thick accent."

"Very thick. And he talked slowly too."

"Like he was having trouble searching for words?" Park then got an idea. "Tell me about your background, son."

"I was born here in Seattle in 2000. Why?"

"Where are your parents from?"

"South Korea."

"Were they born in the US also?"

"No, they came over from Inchon in 1995."

"My parents immigrated here from there, too. I know that even though the Anglos here can't figure out our origins easily, quite often, us first-generation Asians can tell what part of Asia others come from because we pick up on subtle appearance or clothing or mannerism differences better."

"I haven't thought about it much, but I can see how you might be right," the clerk said.

"So, do you think you could tell where he came from?"

"I don't know. I haven't thought about it."

"Give me your first impression, best guess, gut feeling," said Park. He knew that gut feelings tended to be right more often than not.

"My first thought is Korea, but he seemed less comfortable here than the other Koreans I know."

"Could he be from North Korea?"

"Whoa, I hadn't thought of that. That would make sense. Yeah, maybe."

"I don't suppose he told you where he was staying, did he?"

"No," answered the kid. "But I know there's a big Korean area in North Seattle near Shoreline. If I was new in town and struggled with the language, I'd want to hang closer to my peeps."

Park was thinking the same thing. "I know where it is. Thanks, you've been a great help."

———

In Bayonne, New Jersey, Paul O'Malley strained to hear sounds. But he couldn't hear anything. He couldn't see anything either. As he moved his head, he realized it was covered by a cloth bag. He shook his head, trying to clear it. He did a quick systems check and realized he was sitting in a chair with his hands handcuffed behind him. His feet were on a hard floor but were secured to the chair legs with what seemed like duct tape. His butt was sore, and his legs were going numb, but his shoulders and wrists were in pain from being stuck in the awkward position for who knows how long. He tried to recall what happened at the meeting. One minute the people were looking at him, and the next, he had a sharp, searing pain behind his right ear, and he saw stars. He didn't remember anything else until just now.

It was still quiet in the room he was in. He understood he was captive. And although he couldn't hear anything, he wasn't sure he was alone in the room. Or there could be cameras focused on him. For thirty minutes, he lowered his head and didn't move much but strained mightily to hear anyone make a sound. After he decided that he was alone in the room, he began to move more. Another ten minutes passed without any sound, so he reached for the back waistband of his pants. *Good*, he thought, *they're still there*. He withdrew a bobby pin from the waistband that was slid behind his belt and, by feel, directed it into the handcuff on his right wrist. He freed it within ten seconds and then sat there for another five minutes, again trying to determine whether he was eliciting a reaction. Once he felt sure no one else was there or coming into the room, he slowly brought his hands to his face and lifted the cloth bag.

He looked around the room. He was on a chair in the middle, and there was another chair in front of him, facing his. There was a closed steel door behind that chair. He let his eyes wander first. The walls were bare, and there were no obvious cameras in the corners in front of him. He slowly turned his head to examine the rest of the room. It was just as bare as the front. There was that single door and no windows. There was nothing he could use as a weapon except the chairs and the handcuffs. A plan started forming in his mind.

It was unlikely that whoever came through the door next would be a friend. That there was an empty chair meant someone wanted to get information from him. Therefore, that person wouldn't just ask a few questions and then send him on his merry way. O'Malley knew he was in for a rough ride at best and might get "disappeared" at worst. He needed to act early while he was still fairly strong, not beaten up further and not weakened by starvation. Above all, he knew that if they took him somewhere else, it would be a very bad prognostic sign for his future.

He began by undoing the cuff on his left wrist with the bobby pin, but he kept the cuffs in his hand. He looked at his feet and was relieved to see duct tape. He had to make whoever came through the door think he was still secured, so he bent down and started tearing the tape from the chair legs behind his ankles. He left the rest stuck to his pants so no one in front of him could see he was free. Once this was done, he stretched his legs to get the blood flowing through them again. Then he quietly stood and went to the door to see if it was locked.

It was. He walked around the rest of the room, looking and feeling closely for any other openings in the walls. There were no windows and only one small air vent near the ceiling opposite the door. There were no secret access doors that he could see. He inhaled deeply through his nose to identify any smells that might help him later. But all he got was the smell of an old building, nothing special.

He went back to the cloth bag he left on the chair and examined the inside. He put it back on and grabbed it from the outside near his eyes. Without releasing that hand, he removed it using the other and used the ratchet of the handcuffs to rub the inside of the bag where his eyes would be. After a few minutes, he put the bag back on.

Yes, he thought. He had removed enough fibers from the inside of the bag that he could now see out well enough. He examined the outside of the bag again and was satisfied that it looked just the same as when it was first put on his head.

With the walk around the room, the numbness had left his legs, so he sat back down on the chair and looked at his feet to make sure they looked like they were still attached to the chair legs. They did, so he put the bag back on his head. He would see the door and the chair in front of him, whether his head was down or looking straight ahead. He then put his hands back behind him, holding the open handcuffs with each hand. No one could see his hands from the front, but if they walked behind him, he would likely be in trouble.

He heard the door handle turn with the telltale sound of a button lock popping open, so he raised his head slowly from its place on his chest and then shook it side to side to feign just regaining consciousness. He hoped his captor would be less guarded if he thought Paul was still foggy. He looked out from inside the bag and saw not one but two men enter and then close the door. He didn't see them relock the door and didn't hear any manipulation of it from outside.

Paul weaved his upper body and head side to side and said weakly, "Who's there?"

One of the men sat in front of him, while the other stood next to the door. They both looked to be in their thirties and reasonably fit. *This is going to be tricky*, he thought.

"Okay, tell me your real name, Paul," said the chair guy. Paul thought he may have been in the meeting room, but he wasn't sure.

Paul knew he had to act quickly to maximize surprise. He continued to weave a little and then replied just above a whisper, so the interrogator had to lean in closer. Paul tried to talk again, quieter this time, and the guy now had his ear next to the front of Paul's face.

Paul quickly grabbed the back of the man's neck with his left hand and used the thin open jaw of the toothed arm of the handcuffs in his right hand to drive forcefully into the man's left ear. The man screamed, and as he reached up to his injured ear, Paul used both hands to slam the man's nose into Paul's knee.

He lost consciousness and fell to the floor, and Paul transitioned to the man by the door, whose eyes were now huge and his mouth wide open. He reached for the door handle, but Paul had exploded out of the chair to hit him as hard as he could, like a linebacker hitting a quarterback. He slammed him against the wall, knocking his breath out. Paul easily spun him to face away from him and applied a rear naked choke. After ten seconds, the man went limp, and Paul held him for another thirty seconds. He figured even if the guy survived, he wouldn't be able to communicate ever again. He then turned his attention back to the first guy, who was now stirring a little. He was bleeding from his left ear and nose, but no blood was on his neck. If he applied the same rear naked choke on this guy, he would get a lot of blood on his clothing, so he achieved the same effect by pressing on both carotid arteries forcefully to cut off the blood supply to the brain. Once the first man was out again, Paul quickly went through their pockets, grabbing their wallets, phones, and folding pocket knives. The man by the door had a small .380 pistol on the back of his waistband. Paul took that, too, shaking his head.

He felt better about his opponents' lack of skill now. He knew that a lot of people gravitated to the smallest pistol they could afford, not really knowing that it was also a lot less effective. He rationalized that even if he couldn't necessarily take someone down with a .380, no one wanted to get shot with one, either.

His next priority was to get out of the room and the building if possible. He stuffed the collected pocket litter into his own pockets and opened the door quietly. No one was on the other side, so he stuck his head out and looked left and right. Empty. He took a chance and headed to the left.

"All right, we have our orders." The legal attaché in Barranquilla was briefing his team, which now included Sam and Tom Jensen. Sam's SAC had given approval for him to stay in Colombia, since valuable time would be wasted getting him back to Seattle, and he was the only FBI agent to have seen the potential intermediary. Plus, Sam thought Tom had good instincts and now also had skills in close-quarters conflict—these, along with his language skills and knowledge of Latin America, could be very helpful.

"We need to find the middle-aged guy in the red shirt who was seen with our perp," said the attaché. "If we find him, we can run him up the flagpole to see what falls out."

The ambassador added, "We will coordinate things out of our consulate here. I will go back to Bogotá shortly but be in constant contact with people here. I will turn over some rocks in Bogotá that might lead to some intel."

"Jensen?" asked the attaché. Both Sam and Tom looked up. "Since you are the only ones to have seen the guy, you have the point on this." The attaché may have been uncomfortable with a civilian being directly involved, but they needed all the help they could get. He gave them each a satellite phone and gave Sam a pistol and an M4 rifle. "You know how to use this?"

"Yessir," they both replied in unison. Sam glanced at Tom from the corner of his eye, wondering what else his nephew hadn't told him about.

The next morning Tom used the consulate's Wi-Fi to call his father free of international charges. He detailed the events so far, including the altercation in Necoclí. "Dad, that stuff you showed me came back to me instantly, like it was instinct!" He was feeling good about his contribution so far.

John, although glad his son was safe, was also concerned. "I didn't know Sam came down there and met you. When he asked for your number, I thought he was just going to call you." While he thought FBI agents were impressive, John realized the reason was that they put themselves in harm's way. It wasn't a stretch to realize that his son would be in harm's way, too. On the other hand, if his son and his brother could help bring to justice the people responsible for this, he would be proud.

"That's awesome, Tom, and I'm glad you're safe. What are you guys going to do next?"

"I'm not exactly sure, but they want us to try to track down the guy that got away. They figure that we are the best people for that since we are the only ones who saw him."

"I understand Sam doing that, but why are they asking a civilian like you to do it?"

"I don't know, Dad, maybe they like not having to pay someone else to do that. Plus, I speak the language and know the area pretty well, and Uncle Sam spent a lot of time talking to them before they agreed to send me with him. How are things at home?"

"Things are starting to get tense now. We're starting to see some shortages of basic foodstuffs."

"Like what?" Tom thought it had only been a few days since the attacks. What could possibly be missing from the store shelves?

"You know we have become a just-in-time society over the last twenty years or so. It's a very complex system that requires every step to perform optimally. If any step breaks down, the whole system breaks down."

"What do you mean by that?" To Tom, the stores were always full, which meant there was always plenty of everything.

His dad answered, "Not many people know this, but the grocery stores each only have about three days' worth of inventory on hand at any one time. And they carry a lot of imported food, from Chilean sea bass to Japanese sake to Mediterranean olive oil. We make a lot of foodstuffs here in North America, but it's not enough to meet the needs of everyone here. Plus, a lot of the stuff we make has foreign contributions. In other words, we need to import certain ingredients to make so-called American products."

"Okay, so what does that mean?"

"It means we're starting to see shortages since the ports have closed. Fortunately, we have enough oil and gas to produce and refine, so products that are in the US can be delivered without too much trouble. But certain industries are starting to feel it. The shelves in the grocery stores are not as full, and there's an underlying sense of concern among shoppers. Hospitals are no different. They also try to decrease their inventory costs as much as possible, and therefore any disruption in the supply chain is a big problem. We had someone die yesterday because the only antibiotic that his infection was susceptible to was made in Switzerland. We'd exhausted our supply, and no other nearby hospitals or distributors had any to give us."

"That's too bad," said Tom, still not understanding the potential depth of the problem.

His dad explained further, "Because of the tremendous economic pressures, our medical product manufacturers have been consolidated to one or two producers for each typical product, whether it be a medicine or a mesh or an artificial joint. Shortages of these in the past have generally been due to production-line disruptions, such as contamination, that can be corrected fairly quickly. And many, many of the things we use in the hospital are disposable, from gauze to syringes to plastic ventilator circuits. If they need products from overseas to make these, that's as good as not having them at all. Can you imagine a hospital not having any ventilators?"

Tom thought for a moment and realized how bad that would be—how many people could die.

His father went on. "This affects millions of people quickly. Now think about the same domino effect with food. People will get desperate and go from asking for help to demanding help to resorting to force to get what they think they deserve. It will affect everyone here, one way or another."

"Wow," Tom said. "I hadn't thought of it that way. I just go down to the corner and get some fresh papaya. I didn't realize the food could run out that fast. It's a good thing you have your garden."

"Yeah, it will be good if we can keep it."

"What do you mean, if you can keep it?"

"Well, you remember what people said about this area when you were growing up, right? People always talked about how our neighborhood had everything. Well, during hard times, when people have nothing, they remember who has plenty. Then they come for it."

"So?" asked Tom.

"So, what happens is first they ask politely, then they plead, then they demand, then they take," explained his dad. "We can't last very long if a big enough group of people decide they want our produce."

"What are you going to do then?"

"It's going to be difficult, but we are going to need to protect our neighborhood by force of arms. We can't depend on the police and sheriff to protect us. They have problems of their own. Fortunately, most of the neighbors are armed to various degrees. We are starting to talk about the best way to do that."

"Oh man, this is really serious," said Tom.

"Yes, it is," replied his father. "If shortages last long enough, then people become savages. It can potentially ruin our nation's entire way of life."

Just then, Sam came in and twirled his finger in the air as a sign for Tom to wrap it up and get going. "I gotta go, Dad. Uncle Sam is leaving. Love you, and be safe."

"I love you back. You be safer," said John.

Sam and Tom walked out together to get into their rental car. They each had bags loaded with not only clothing and toiletries but also the radios, extra batteries, knives, body armor, firearms, and ammo to go with them.

"What was that about?" Sam asked.

"I was just talking to Dad. I hope that's okay," he added after a pause, worried that he might not be authorized to talk to him.

"Sure, it's fine," replied Sam, who picked up on Tom's concern. "Everyone in the world knows we're looking for the perpetrators of the attacks, anyway, all over the world. Just don't tell him exactly where you are from now on, okay?"

"Fair enough. I was filling him in on you and me and what we've done so far. He was pretty upset at first since he didn't know you were coming down here, much less that we would get into stuff together."

They climbed into the now-dusty rental car with Sam behind the wheel. As he put it in gear, Sam pressed further. "How are things back in Texas?"

Tom related the details and said, "I didn't realize things—like food and medical supplies—could start running out so soon."

Sam answered, "Yeah, that could be a big problem if this lasts for any length of time like it's shaping up to. It's a good thing your dad likes to be prepared. Is he worried about running out of food?"

"Not food so much since he has the gardens and greenhouse. They've also got several buckets of freeze-dried and dehydrated food. Plus, Mom gets a big supply of meat from the kids at the county livestock show every year, so they're good with food. But he also told me about how once people run out of stuff, they start looking for where they can get it. If they realize Mom and Dad have what they don't, they will come for it."

"That doesn't sound good. Do they have a plan for that?"

"Oh, yeah. You know Dad, Mr. Plan A, B, C, D, and E himself."

"I know my brother," Sam said, nodding, as he continued to navigate uphill on the crowded streets of Barranquilla. "So what's his plan?"

"If it comes to it, he has plenty of guns and knows how to use them."

"How does he know about firearms? He is so busy with work, and we didn't have any at home growing up."

"He realized a few years ago that as he got older, he would become more of a target for bad guys to take advantage of. He explained that's the way it has always been for every species as long as there has been life on earth."

Sam chuckled. "That sounds like him. So he bought a gun."

"Not only that, he realized that he needed to know how to use it, so he got regular training from the best people he could find. He will travel hours to train with Marines and cops who have been 'deep in the shit,' as he calls it. He tells me about it sometimes, shooting with his opposite hand, from awkward positions, moving while shooting, clearing malfunctions, and reloading one-handed, with either hand, using a pistol and a rifle. Pretty cool stuff. He even said he passed the FBI agent pistol qualification at one of his courses."

"He never told me that! That test isn't exactly easy."

"He probably didn't tell you because he was mad he didn't pass the Instructor level. You know how he is."

Sam laughed again, remembering his brother's competitive streak. "That's probably exactly why he didn't tell me. What about the close-quarters stuff you did in Necoclí? You said he taught you some things. How did he know about those? I know firearms instructors don't usually delve into that."

"Well, he said that as he got more and more into the firearms training, he realized that there were a lot of limitations on their use and that people who would attack him would likely do it as more of a close-in ambush than announce it from a few yards away. He went and got some training in that, too. He said he may be a dinosaur, but dinosaurs have teeth, too, and he was going to use them if he needed to."

"Damn, I had no idea." His respect for his older brother just increased a couple of notches.

"Ahh, there," Sam said, pointing at a street sign that read Calle 19. He turned east. "This is also Route 90, the main belt road through town." The divided road was lined with dusty tire shops, small appliance repair shops, and the like, crowding in on both sides.

Tom changed the subject. "So, where are we going anyway?"

"We are going to chase bad guys. You up for it?"

NINE

SAN CRISTOBAL, VENEZUELA. Rodrigo Ramirez was sitting alone at a table in a small house in a rough quarter of town in front of his handler.

"I am very disappointed in you," said the handler. Ramirez didn't know his name or even where he was from. His features were equal part Caucasian and Asian, with coal-black eyes that pierced straight through him. He couldn't place the man's accent either. His pulse quickened as he anticipated the handler's wrath.

Yet the man was calm, which paradoxically made Ramirez very nervous. "Tell me everything," the handler said.

Ramirez detailed his lunch with the Colombians, how they made their tail, and their foiled ambush.

"Why did you run? You are supposed to be a professional."

"There were two of them tailing us, both younger and faster and stronger than me, and they obviously had skills. They quickly disabled the other two. I knew that if they caught me, I would be tortured until I gave up information."

"And so you came straight to me. Now they are coming here."

"No, señor. I made sure no one followed me. I didn't even use my real name with the other two. They think my last name is Rodriguez."

"Clever," said the handler. He knew that the Americans had capabilities to track people that didn't require humans on the ground. He came to a decision. "You are dismissed now, Rodrigo. We will have more for you soon."

Ramirez was relieved. He stood up and walked to the front door.

"Not that way. The back door," said the man. "I don't want anyone on the street seeing you leave this house."

"I understand," said Ramirez, and he changed direction. As he put his hand on the rear doorknob, the man shot him in the back of the head. It was just another gunshot in the rough part of town, arousing no suspicion.

Then the handler walked out the front door and got into his dusty brown car.

———

"We've got a second subject leaving the house. We'll call him Subject B," said the National Security Agency (NSA) technician looking at the monitor of the satellite feed. "He's getting into a brown two-door beater. No sign of Subject A leaving yet."

"Roger that," said the shift supervisor, who picked up the telephone and punched a speed-dial button. "We have more activity at the house. Second subject leaving," he said to the voice at the other end.

Nancy Anderson, the thirty-nine-year-old chief of the Data Acquisition section of the Signals Intelligence Directorate at the NSA, strode into the National Security Operations Center. She had been contacted immediately after the Information Need (IN) signal was sent from the consulate in Barranquilla, which in turn activated it after Sam called in his status immediately after getting his prisoner into his vehicle. She was the one who was able to backtrack the satellite data that had been observing the northern coastal area of Colombia on the day and time of the incident.

The area to be searched was fairly small, and because the incident occurred in the open, they eventually found a group of five men on a street corner, which became four and then one lying down. This corresponded to the description of the event, so she used Wrangler to sift through the telecommunications data for that area while she tried to visually track the man who ran away. Unfortunately, he'd run straight to the bus station.

The bus station had a cover for the passengers, protecting them from the rain and the sun while entering and exiting the buses. Visual evidence of the man leaving was no longer an option. So Chief Anderson used the massive computing power of the NSA to search for all the known language variations for the words "help," "compromised," "leaving," "operation," "assistance," and "location" that were either spoken into or texted into a mobile phone in the area of the bus station, and then along the routes of all buses that left the station over the next twelve hours. This was a gargantuan task and required an all-hands-on-deck effort from the Signals Intelligence (SigInt) division, which also had to surreptitiously access the network of the largest telecom company in Colombia, Telefónica Telecom.

The division ultimately identified 132 telephones that had used one of those keywords. They set about to track them backward in time and found that 59 of them fell within the triangulated area of the three closest cell phone towers at the time and place of the event with Sam and Tom. They then focused on the subsequent communications of all 59 of those phones' owners. They quit using keywords and devoted all their attention to evaluating everything they could about the outgoing and incoming communications, whether voice or text or social media, as well as the name and address of the owners and every person they communicated with.

Any communication that didn't fit the context of what an average person would say was then examined more intensely. Ultimately, Nancy's team found five phones that met the additional suspicion trigger and focused all their attention on them. One by one, they identified by satellite visualization the people changing their mode of transportation and were able to rule out four of them based on different physical appearances from the man who ran away. One matched, and he was tracked to San Cristobal, Venezuela, and entered the house they were currently watching.

SigInt's attention was now focused on the man leaving in the old brown car. They tracked him via satellite while they repeated the process of evaluating all the electronic communications in the area. Over the next two hours of cross-referencing location data of mobile phones with the man's physical location, they were able to identify his cell phone number. It was registered to a prepaid phone that had been sold out of a kiosk in San Cristobal two weeks earlier.

The momentum of the chase seemed to be lost until they traced all the communications to and from that phone over that previous two-week period. Now it became interesting, because there were only 163 communications during that time frame, involving seventy-eight unique locations. Many of these locations were mundane ones that everyone contacted to conduct normal activities of daily living—restaurants, utility companies, three different women, car repair shops, and the like.

But there was one location the man accepted and made calls to that didn't exist when cross-referenced by the NSA techs. That immediately set off red flags for Anderson and her team and was quickly shot up the chain to Secretary of Defense Donaldson. He coordinated with the director of national intelligence, who surveyed his available assets nearby to see who could get to San Cristobal the fastest.

———

"How do you feel about going to Venezuela?" Sam asked Tom as he got off the satellite phone.

"Oh, shit, that's the one place Dad told me to avoid," said Tom.

"Well, it seems that the higher-ups were able to electronically track our guy, who had escaped all the way across Colombia to a town in Venezuela called San Cristobal, near the border. They say we are the closest people to that location. They are currently also tracking another guy associated with him. This is likely to get very difficult. We'll need to stay unseen to all authorities in a hostile country while searching for a needle in a haystack. If you don't want to go, I understand. I'll put you on the next plane out of Bogotá to wherever you want to go."

Tom thought about it for a few seconds. "Difficult? It could be worse. We could be navigating completely unknown territory for over two years, rowing and poling boats upriver, then crossing snowy mountains in thin moccasins, braving rapids and grizzly bears, like our ancestor Willard did on the Lewis and Clark expedition."

"Yeah, they had a rough ride."

"Plus, I know the language and the people and the customs better than you do. I can't leave you alone to try to learn that stuff while you're also chasing the bad guys. Let's go."

"Are you sure? I don't want to run afoul of your dad."

"Me neither, and yes, he will be pissed, but he's not here. And something tells me that if it was him instead of me, he would be saying the same thing I just did. Let me find San Cristobal on the map so I can help you navigate."

———

Chuck Haggard endured the stream of colleagues coming to his office to offer their condolences and help with anything he might need. He politely said all the right things and accepted the hugs from the men and women who truly cared for him, all the while thinking he really just wanted to get back to the job of finding his wife's killer and dealing him the utmost justice he deserved.

Once his human sympathy chain came to an end, he placed his head in his hands for a minute to collect his thoughts and then stood up from his desk and walked out to the wardroom where his unit did their office work.

His human trafficking unit consisted of about fifty men and women, about two-thirds of whom were analysts and investigators, and the rest were the "point of the spear" types, the ones who got called to put their lives on the line to break up cells identified by their colleagues. One of the things the analysts and investigators did was scour the "dark web," an area where people went to hide their electronic activities from the authorities. Regular citizens were not able to penetrate the dark web because of its multilayered security thresholds that had to be passed to enter, but bad guys talk to each other as they conduct illicit activities. New York City was a hub for international human trafficking, and therefore his unit was very good at finding and apprehending the perpetrators. Before assuming leadership of the team, Chuck had worked all three sections for a few years each and was intimately familiar with the capabilities of all of them. His people knew this and loved him for the fact that he was a worker like them, not a political ass-kisser. Plus, he was a family man who'd just lost his wife. They were about as mad as he was.

Chuck stood on the platform that overlooked the wardroom and cleared his throat.

"I want to thank all of you for your kind words and offers to help over the last few days. It means more to me than you will ever know. This has been the hardest thing I have ever had to do, and as a proud member of one of the elite units of the finest police force in the world, I keep reminding myself of what our training and experience have taught us in difficult times like this. When things get really tough, and you can't see a way out or even where to start looking, you go back to the basics. For us, the basics are kicking over every rock to find the bad guys and then kicking their asses straight back to hell where they belong."

He saw heads nodding in encouragement.

"So, I've been thinking. You men and women are truly the best in the world at finding evil people like the ones that did this series of attacks. The feds have their hands full, but they can't attend to everything. And even though they are good at searching for political-type terrorists, they don't have the experience that we do in terms of searching for under-world figures. They don't know the places they frequent on the web and in person or the people they hang out with. We can contribute to that search in a way that they probably haven't even thought of yet.

"I would therefore like to ask anyone interested to see what you can do in terms of finding these people and bringing them to justice. I know it is not in our traditional mission of human trafficking, but I think we are the best agency positioned to help with this. I am not ordering any-one to do this, but any volunteers would be greatly appreciated. I'll deal with the brass if any heat comes from there."

Rufus Johnson, Chuck Haggard's right-hand man leading the unit, stood up. Chuck had known Rufus since he was a beat cop in the South Bronx and was there the day Rufus got the call that his thirteen-year-old daughter had been abducted. Her body was found six months later on a Caribbean island.

"Boss, everyone here is deeply sorry for what you have had to deal with. And I'd like to be the first to tell you that you are behind the curve on this."

Chuck's eyes narrowed, and he clenched his teeth. He was not used to being behind the curve on anything.

Rufus went on, "This entire unit dropped everything and has been working day and night ever since this happened to find these bastards."

Chuck's eyes un-narrowed and then filled with tears. He unclenched his teeth, swallowed hard, and wanted to say something but couldn't find the words. *God, I love these people.*

TEN

"MIERDE," SAID GELLERT INTO THE PHONE. His parents in the old country wanted their baby boy to be strong, like a spear, so they gave him a name that meant exactly that in their native tongue. Gellert was the only child born of the union between a senior communist apparatchik in charge of monitoring telecommunications in Hungary after the failed coup in 1956 and his Olympic javelin-thrower wife from the same town as he. Gellert's father was a True Believer in every sense of the word, and his mother benefited from the extra attention that communists afforded Olympic athletes, so they both instilled in their son an appreciation for not only forced collectivization but also the subtle skill of ingratiation that almost always led to an easier life behind the iron curtain.

Gellert Demyan was strong, a natural athlete, intelligent, and ambitious—traits that generally lead to success in all parts of the world. He ultimately landed in the Hungarian Intelligence Service and learned the skills of recruiting and managing teams of assets, both willing and otherwise, from the Soviet overlords, the KGB. It was there that he learned Spanish, Farsi, and Mandarin Chinese, in addition to the usual espionage skills. He gave 100 percent to every mission he was assigned, and he was successful in completing them 80 percent of the time—an unheard-of success rate in the espionage field.

After the fall of the Soviet Union and its allies in Eastern Europe, Gellert was suddenly unemployed and without a mission. He still believed that capitalism was evil and the sole cause of all the injustice in the world, so he found the only man in Hungary who not only shared that vision but, more importantly, could also finance the efforts to bring it down.

He had surreptitiously arranged to be seated at a table in a Viennese café next to Piotr Gyure several years ago and attracted the man's attention by speaking Hungarian-accented German to the server. They struck up a conversation and, as new acquaintances often do, began to commiserate about problems both local and global. Gyure was pleasantly surprised to find a younger man who seemed to share his outlook on some of the world's problems and arranged regular café visits over the next few months. He had been looking for a man he could mentor in continuing his life's work and finally decided that Gellert Demyan was it.

Gyure had made his money over the years using capitalism's tools for his purposes. He was particularly gifted at recognizing patterns in the various financial markets and rode the momentum waves like a champion surfer. Once he got big enough, he realized he could move the markets himself, so he did and became even more wealthy than he ever imagined.

In his heart, though, Gyure was still fighting the battles from his childhood, where his family was a victim of the Nazis imposing their irrational view of the world by force onto the masses under their control. That force included the ability to enter their home whenever they wanted and rape his mother and little sister for several hours one night. His sister was never the same after that. She hardly ate, quit interacting with everyone, became as malnourished as any concentration camp inhabitant, and finally died a year later.

He, therefore, had a deep distrust of most governments; the bigger, the more dangerous, he thought. He also saw the rise of huge corporations and the resulting incestuous relationships with governments to be a major contributor to the oppression of more and more people.

Over the next few years of his employment by Gyure, Demyan was given increasing responsibility for managing the older man's affairs. He accomplished his tasks with complete focus, often enhancing the returns more than expected. During this time, he traveled extensively all over the world, meeting people that could be force multipliers in Gyure's overall goals of eventually reducing the massive power of the world's largest governments and corporations.

Because of his language skills, he naturally spent a lot of time in Persia, China, and South and Central America. Among the thousands of people that he met for business over the years was Nikolai Khobulin. Born and raised in Uzbekistan, he was tapped at a young age by the KGB to help with their efforts to destabilize the governments of Nicaragua and then Bolivia. For the last few years, Khobulin had been in Venezuela, trying to keep the current socialist dictator in power. He also had a side hustle earning extra coin by helping Gellert Demyan with whatever he needed. He was now calling Demyan to tell him about the dead man in his former house in San Cristobal.

"You know the Americans are probably tracing this call right now, don't you?" asked Demyan.

"I figured they were tracing Ramirez, so I left immediately. But they don't know this phone number."

"Don't be so sure," replied Demyan. "For all we know, they have a drone that you can't see or hear that is following you even as we speak."

———

The Americans didn't have a drone fixed on them yet, but they were preparing to launch one from the nearest naval ship in the southern Caribbean. The USS *Georgia* was an Ohio-class ballistic missile submarine that was converted to a cruise missile submarine after the START II treaty, which limited the number of nuclear missiles that the United States and USSR possessed. Prior to the treaty, it carried twenty-four ballistic nuclear missiles. Afterward, it carried a maximum of 154 Tomahawk cruise missiles, but American engineers were very creative in using the vertical launch tubes for many other missions, including drone launches. It was currently moving silently submerged north of the island of Aruba, and the captain issued orders to its resident SEAL team to begin preparations to launch out of one of its forward torpedo tubes to retrieve the drone after its mission was completed.

Nancy Anderson's team at the NSA had been furiously crunching the data to get a fix on the location of the new phone while their DOJ liaison was keeping the FBI headquarters abreast of their progress in near-real time. There was only a short delay of a few minutes before that information was relayed to Sam and Tom, who were rapidly approaching the eastern border of Colombia on their way to San Cristobal.

Meanwhile, the CIA liaison was also relaying the same information to headquarters in Langley, which had a team working on identifying the person connected to the phone number and the house that it originated from.

"Nikolai Khobulin," announced the junior member of Anderson's NSA team. "The phone is registered to Nicolas Cobos, but after deep-diving into the provenance of the registration and cross-referencing it to the names of known foreign agents and their arrival into the area, I was able to connect it ultimately to Khobulin, an Uzbeki foreign agent that has been active in Latin America for the last five years."

"Great, where is he?" asked Anderson, ever the pragmatist. She instantly decided that the information they had acquired was not coincidental.

"Working on it, boss," replied the chief technician in charge of real time localization. "He is currently heading generally northeast, toward the town of Merida. And the location data from the phone is generally tracking the location of the brown car on satellite."

"Do you have a street or highway name?" asked Anderson.

"T-07," replied the tech. Anderson consulted her map of Venezuela. This road led to Merida and then ultimately to Caracas, which made sense intuitively to her.

"What assets do we have in the area?" she asked the team of DOJ, CIA, State, and DOD liaisons. Two minutes later, she had the hard-copy printouts of the closest assets of the respective agencies that might help apprehend the owner of the phone.

"Sam and Tom Jensen," she said to the group, but chiefly to the DOJ liaison. "It says here that Tom is a civilian and related to the FBI agent. How on earth can that possibly help us right now?"

"Apparently, he was instrumental in initially locating the people who were responsible for the Port of Houston attack, and he kept his uncle from getting killed in Colombia," replied the DOJ liaison. "The ambassador there okayed his participation since he also knows the language and the culture of the area. His uncle is from the Seattle Field Office and wouldn't be able to navigate the area on his own."

"Fair enough," she sighed. "We also have the USS *Georgia* north of Aruba, and CIA has their standard element at the embassies of Colombia, Brazil, and Guyana. I can't order any of these assets to act, so we need to bump this up . . . fast."

Her boss, Stan Inaka, was the son of a Japanese POW from the 1944 Battle of Saipan, who was a captain in the Intelligence section of his unit. The information he provided directly led to the success of the Allies in that battle, which was thought by many to be the turning point in the war. After the battle, he was shipped directly to Fort Hunt in Virginia for further interrogation. Once the war was over several months later, he was offered the option to stay in the United States. It wasn't a difficult decision to make. He chose to stay in Virginia and ultimately married and raised a family. His son Stan must have inherited the genetic predisposition for intelligence gathering and was hired by the NSA in the 1970s and steadily rose through the ranks. He now was the director of the Signals Intelligence Directorate, and by the time Nancy Anderson was finishing her sentence, he was already on the phone with his boss, the director of the NSA.

"Hang on, let me have you give that info to the SecDef, who's right here," said the director.

"I got it," said David Donaldson after talking to Inaka, who then relayed the info to the rest of the Security Council. In one minute, the orders were placed to reorient the Jensens and the crew of the *Georgia* to the new information. The total time from acquiring Khobulin's name to the relay to the Jensens and the submarine was less than fifteen minutes.

ELEVEN

PAUL O'MALLEY HAD ESCAPED from the building in New Jersey, made his way back to the FBI field office, and reported to his SAC. His team had subsequently raided the building, but it was empty, and the forensics team was systematically going through it looking for helpful evidence. Needless to say, he could not go back to the area where he had first met the 415 people, so his boss put his recent experience through the New York State Intelligence Center, a fusion center created by the Department of Homeland Security in the wake of September 11 in hopes of connecting the dots that different agencies might dredge up but couldn't put together individually.

All the relevant law enforcement agencies in a given area had representatives at their respective fusion centers. In New York, the Intelligence Center was in Latham, outside of Albany. The NYPD had a representative there, of course, and recognized Paul's location and recent events. His bosses had already noticed the involvement of Chuck Haggard's unit and were not only *not* mad but actively encouraged their pursuits because they wanted a piece of the action—and, they hoped, the glory at the end.

So Paul got tasked with the human trafficking division of the NYPD. He was initially upset because he didn't see the connection between human trafficking and the destruction of the world's trade system, but after he learned of Chuck Haggard's sad story of losing his wife on the cruise ship, he was all in on his new assignment. His new teammates were happy to have another member who could not only gather and analyze intelligence but also, obviously, act on it as well.

One of the Trafficking Unit's first leads was generated from the team member responsible for the Russian-language dark websites. One of the benefits of being part of a force of over forty thousand people was that there were people from all backgrounds and countries. Ivan Popov was born in Kursk, near the Ukrainian border, and moved with his parents to New York when he was twelve. He knew the language, of course, but more importantly, he knew the culture and how things worked there. He even remembered the stories of the notorious criminals from his time there, as well as the new ones he was encountering.

Ivan knocked and entered Chuck's office. "Boss, do you remember Andrei Chikatilo?"

"I've heard the name, but remind me of the details."

"He was a Russian serial killer from Ukraine, actually near where I grew up, who raped, tortured, and killed young teenage girls. He admitted to fifty-six of them."

"So where is he now?" Chuck thought an evil person like that could easily kill thousands on a cruise ship.

"That's just it. He was executed by the state in 1994 after he got caught. But there's a person who uses that name on the dark web."

Chuck raised his eyebrows. "And?"

"It turns out that Andrei has been communicating with a known 415 leader named Jack Upshaw."

Chuck focused his eyes on Ivan. "Go get Paul O'Malley and bring him in here so you can brief the both of us."

———

"Yessir, on our way. I'll keep you updated," said Sam Jensen to his ultimate boss, Frank Burroughs, who had called him directly with his new assignment. Sam had left the coast road, and the men were now in farm country, with fields of fruits and vegetables interspersed with a few small plots of sheep and goats.

He hung up. "Wow, I don't know how many field agents the director calls personally, but I can safely say this is the first time I've ever been called by one," said Sam.

"And?" said Tom, who thought it was obviously more efficient to do it this way.

"He said we are looking for an older, somewhat beat-up brown two-door car on the road T-07 from San Cristobal to Merida, Venezuela. Can you look up where that is in relation to us and what would be the best way to get there, and how long it might take?"

"Gimme a sec," said Tom while he consulted the navigation app on his phone.

"Okay, we are just east of Macaio and close to the Venezuela border. Since we are along the coast and they are heading to Merida in the mountains, I would suggest after we cross the border, we cross the mouth of Lake Maracaibo and head in the general direction of Caracas. It will take us a few hours to get to a point where we can either continue to Caracas or pivot up to Merida if he stays there."

Sam replied, "That makes sense. The only issue is that my FBI credentials probably won't help me get across the border checkpoint."

"I already thought of that, and I've checked the Google satellite map. It looks like there is a dirt road that skirts the main road that crosses the border. You get to it via a back road in the little town on this side. There are buildings and cars on the dirt road on the map, and it doesn't look like there are any other border control points along it. It curls back to the main road a couple of miles inside Venezuela. Convenient for smugglers, I'm sure."

"Let's get gas before we cross the border," said Sam. "I don't know how much we'll have on the other side." He knew that even though Venezuela was formerly one of the great oil-producing countries of the world, its inept government over the years led to a critical shortage of refined products. If he and Tom ran out of gas, their mission was over.

Sam then relayed the plan to Director Burroughs. Normally, they would have had the availability of air assets, which would shorten the pursuit time immensely. However, Venezuela still had an Air Force actively patrolling its borders, denying entry to any unauthorized aircraft.

Two hours later, they had successfully inserted themselves into Venezuela and were heading toward Maracaibo. By that time, the drone had launched from the *Georgia*. It had stealth capabilities that protected it from detection by the Venezuelan Air Force and could stay on station for several hours. Once airborne, it was controlled from the Remotely Piloted Aircraft Center at Creech AFB in Nevada. It was smaller than the standard MQ-9 Reaper drones that had seen extensive duty in the Middle East, and it was solely a surveillance and targeting platform.

Armed with state-of-the-art visual and electronic sensors, it could identify targets as small as a paperback book and lock on that target like a police dog on a criminal. The coordinates could then be relayed to the nearest combatant ship with the latest guided missile technology if forceful action was required. Tomahawk cruise missiles got a lot of action in the Middle East from naval vessels, including submarines. That technology was then scaled down to provide the force that could limit the damage to a target as small as a motorcycle traveling at high speed. Guided by the invisible laser, the mark never knew it was being targeted until after it was destroyed.

Because the drone had such advanced technology, capture by hostile forces was unacceptable. Even the pieces of the crashed special forces helicopter in Osama bin Laden's compound in Afghanistan allowed the Chinese to leapfrog their helicopter capabilities in a short period. And even though it was launched by a submarine, it could not be recovered by one. The SEALs were deployed to recover it. It was small, so it didn't need a lot of room to land, but it couldn't land in the jungle. During infiltration, the controllers examined areas open enough to land in but secluded enough to avoid detection but still easy enough for the SEAL team to access and exfiltrate from. Once the LZ was identified, the coordinates were sent to the SEAL team to retrieve it.

Once they had the mission coordinates, the SEALs exited the *Georgia* using the Shallow Water Combat Submersible (SWCS). The successor to the SEAL Delivery Vehicle (SDV) was basically a mini-submarine with a capacity for six SEALs—a pilot, copilot, and four mission-tasked operators and their gear. The SWCS was a dry environment inside, which greatly increased the ability of the team to complete their mission since they didn't have to deal with the added stress of the water exposure for however long it took to get them onto land.

It took two hours for the team to reach the most promising landing point at the southeast quadrant of the Gulf of Venezuela. Multiple rivers emptied into this area, forming estuaries unsuitable for construction, and tidal flats provided a suitable place for the drone to land. The SEALs had to be prepared to defend themselves and to survive for three days in case their position was compromised, or they had to alter the retrieval point, or their exfiltration was delayed. Plus, they had to swim underwater with this gear after they left the SWCS. The drone was designed to be quickly broken down to fit into two large watertight duffel bags that they would also take back to the sub, where technicians could re-task it for another mission within four hours if necessary. The submarine carried four such drones so that they could provide nearly twenty-four-hour coverage of a given area for days if necessary.

Sam and Tom didn't know all this, of course. All they knew was the verbal communication they received via their satellite phone. They were heading toward Barquisimeto and didn't see the drone heading south far above their heads.

TWELVE

"ALL RIGHT, THEN, WHAT DO YOU want me to do?" Said Khobulin to Demyan while driving north toward Merida.

Demyan thought, *Run off the nearest tall bridge*, but didn't say it out loud. He knew that no matter how damaged the vehicle and its occupant may become, the Americans would ultimately be able to piece it together enough to trace it back to him. He needed to find a way to either completely absorb Khobulin or completely eliminate him. Either route would snuff out the trail leading to him if he did it right. As rich as his boss was, he didn't have the ability to vaporize someone thousands of miles away as the Americans had. That left the riskier option.

"Let me work on it," said Demyan. "We have friends in Caracas, so head there for now. I'll let you know soon what the plan will be."

"Okay, thanks," said Khobulin, who nervously scanned the sky for small objects. The remark about the drone had gotten to him.

He had a right to worry. Although the drone was still out of sight, it was headed in his general direction.

———

"Where are we with locating that vehicle?" Nancy Anderson asked her team.

"We are now patched in to the Creech UAV center, and it is now feet dry heading south toward the estimated position of the phone signal," said the technician watching the feed from Creech AFB.

Anderson had a hunch. "Let's ask Sentient to check for unusual activity in and around Caracas."

"Roger that, ma'am."

The armed forces were tied into the Sentient system, which was recently developed to integrate electronic information from not only all governmental sources but many private and commercial sources as well. The US military operates over 150 satellites, and there are dozens more commercial satellites that also collect visual, telephonic, and electronic information. There is virtually no square inch on earth that is not currently being examined every minute of every day. Sentient gathers all this information and analyzes it in near-real time. Once it identifies a particular object or person, it can then analyze the many other variables to see if there is a change in their baseline patterns that may indicate a response to the original object.

"How soon for the UAV to get to the area in question?" asked Anderson, referring to an unmanned aerial vehicle.

"Twenty-three minutes, ma'am," answered the technician.

"Any change in the vector of the phone signal?"

"No, ma'am, we are examining the signals from the local mobile telephone company, and he has gone through Merida heading toward Barquisimeto—estimated time to reach that city is thirty minutes."

"That's cutting it close," said Inaka, standing next to Anderson. He knew it would become much more difficult to pick out a vehicle among thousands of others, especially if buildings and tunnels were involved. It also greatly increased the ability to change cars without being seen, for instance, in a parking garage. And if the guy ditched his phone, US intelligence would be dead in the water.

"Yes, let's hope there aren't many vehicles on that stretch of road when the drone gets there," she answered. "That would make identification much easier."

They watched the feed from the drone on one large monitor, an overlay of its position on a map of Colombia on another, and an estimated position of the phone in question on another map. They used triangulation to estimate its location from area cell towers, but it was only accurate to a radius of about two miles. This position was therefore represented by a shaded circle that corresponded to the best guess given the technological limits.

The controllers at Creech AFB also had access to Sentient and were watching the same feeds as Anderson and her team. They knew the objective and could adjust the flight vectors more quickly if they were looking at the same data. They were, in fact, making minor adjustments periodically based on the changes in the speed of the target circle.

———

Lieutenant Rafael Enriquez was piloting the Venezuelan Air Force Beechcraft King Air, transporting his colonel from his home base in Maracaibo to Caracas for a meeting with his higher-ups. Colonel Alberto Flores did not know the reason he was summoned, but the brass was jumpy, to say the least, and he was worried about the future of his job. The aircraft was climbing eastward through 5,000 feet out of Maracaibo when Enriquez saw a transient fleck of black across a cloud several thousand feet above him. It was late in the afternoon, and the sun was behind him. He pointed it out to his colonel, sitting in the right seat, who also thought it was odd. As Flores contemplated the potential causes, they saw it again, but this time it was present for about fifteen seconds, long enough to see it change its position across the cloud, going from north to south.

Flores had been flying in this area for years and knew that this was out of the standard air traffic patterns. It didn't look like a bird, and he could think of no other flying object besides another aircraft, so he keyed his mike, "Maracaibo Center, VAF 31 climbing east through 7,000 feet approximately twenty-five miles northwest of Carora."

He knew the broken cloud cover was from 10,000 to 15,000 feet. "Do you have any aircraft heading south toward Carora at ten to fifteen thousand feet?"

The senior controller on duty, who was responsible for all the aircraft, military and civilian, in the Maracaibo area of air operations, quickly consulted his monitors. He knew the colonel's voice—everyone did. "No, sir, we have no aircraft flying south at any altitude in that sector."

"Roger that." Flores considered the possibilities. His country's leaders were pounding the war drums, but he knew they had been doing that for the last few years to distract the masses from the real problems of their incompetent leadership. He could see through their propaganda but tried not to rock the boat because his family needed him to keep his job. Not only that, but people who crossed the big bosses frequently got "disappeared," and he hated the thought of his wife and kids being forced to do less than savory things to be able to eat. Those stories of people less fortunate than he were becoming more and more common. He was worried that his underlying attitude toward the leaders, while he worked hard to keep it under wraps, may have been noticed and may have been the reason he was being summoned to Caracas.

Despite the leader's bombastic speech, he also knew the Americans were ratcheting up their language against Venezuela. He was a student of history and knew that a change in language by political leaders was frequently associated with hidden activities designed to undermine the targets in various ways. He made a decision that he hoped would help him keep his job.

"Maracaibo Center, VAF 31. We are breaking from our flight plan to pursue an unauthorized aircraft southbound heading toward Carora." Lieutenant Enriquez banked the plane to the right.

Colonel Flores was counting on the paranoia of the leaders to latch onto any evidence, either real or perceived, of a violation of the sovereignty of the Venezuelan state. He calculated the risk of not finding anything incriminating and decided that it didn't matter if they found anything or not. The leaders would milk the story for all its worth, and they would recognize the value that Flores provided. He said into the mike, "Please notify headquarters and request they ready the Su-30."

"Roger that, Colonel," came the response.

The Venezuelan Air Force only contained nineteen aircraft, ranging from helicopters to transport aircraft to fighter jets, and they were sourced from countries around the world. They had acquired the Sukhoi Flanker-C air superiority fighter in 1996 from Russia, and the leaders kept it at Caracas Air Base to help protect the capital from the evil Americans.

Flores knew he had a slim chance of finding anything using the King Air, but he planned to spend about thirty minutes searching to bolster his standing.

———

"Chief, we may have a problem," announced the SigInt technician to Nancy Anderson. "Sentient has detected an unusual change in the flight pattern of a Venezuelan Air Force plane to head in the same vector as our UAV. They are now on a parallel vector two miles off the UAV's right flank but at a different speed. They are about fifty knots faster than the UAV."

"Creech UAV control here," said the female voice from the loud-speaker. "We are watching the Sentient feed also, and we believe that because the difference in speed is so great, either they don't see the UAV or maybe the plane can't fly much slower."

"You guys are the pilots, so I'll defer to you. But if they can't see it, why did they change vectors?"

"We're still working on that. It is daytime still, so maybe they got lucky and saw it briefly. We can't think of any other reason for them to change vectors like that. Do you guys have any chatter that may give us a clue?"

"Not yet, but we're working on that too," replied Anderson.

"Chief, we have more unusual activity," announced another techni-cian in Anderson's team. "A Venezuelan Sukhoi Su-30 fighter jet is being prepped for flight. They usually only fly at 10:00 a.m. for about ninety minutes, then return to base in Caracas for the rest of the day."

"That sounds ominous," said Anderson. "What are our options?"

Stan Inaka weighed in. "We really need a hard confirmation match-ing the phone signal with the vehicle it's in, if at all possible. Otherwise, we may never find this guy."

"Roger that," said the Creech controller. "We'll continue to vector toward the suspected target, which is about ten minutes away now. If we break off and change direction suddenly, he may see us again anyway."

———

Enriquez and Flores were scanning the sky around them, searching for the phantom speck. Enriquez, with his younger eyes, saw it first at his 9 o'clock and about two thousand feet above him, but he realized he was overtaking it. He throttled down immediately to try to match the speed and realized he was dangerously close to stalling. He then banked to the left and throttled up to keep the aircraft in sight and to avoid stalling. He pointed it out to Flores, saying, "See that black speck against the cloud? It is actually a shadow cast by the aircraft that is barely visible a few hundred yards to the right of the cloud."

Flores followed his outstretched finger, squinting hard, finally saying, "I got it. Sure looks small, though."

"Sí, Colonel." Enriquez thought so too but, because of his relative inexperience, didn't trust his intuition enough to say it out loud first. "If it is so small, then, what could it be?"

"It is obviously a powered aircraft that wasn't detected by our military radar in Maracaibo. I don't know of any commercial drones that have this kind of range or altitude capability." Flores thought further. "The only thing I can imagine is that it's a foreign entity. Who has stealth technology besides the Americans?" But he realized it didn't matter. This was a foreign incursion into Venezuelan airspace and needed a response.

They were now within radio range of Caracas Air Base, so he keyed his mike. "Caracas, VAF 31. We are visually tracking an unauthorized aircraft that is not detected by radar, heading south toward the town of Carora. Request launch of the Su-30 to intercept."

"Copy that, VAF 31." The controller looked at his officer in charge, who nodded. "Launching now."

THIRTEEN

DEMYAN WAS WORKING HARD TRYING to deal with Khobulin. He couldn't use the phones because he knew it was only a matter of time before the Americans could trace the rat line to him and from there to all associates he called. So he had to use surreptitious messages left on forums using aliases to contact his people in Caracas.

Piotr Gyure had insisted that Demyan cultivate people on both sides of the government everywhere he had interests. He believed in covering all his bets so that if any particular government was overthrown, he had a backup plan. He used the government contacts, well-lubricated, of course, to either facilitate or look the other way as necessary for any actions he wanted to be done. If the government stayed in power, he would still have access. He even cultivated the criminal element in every society because they were the ones who were not afraid to use violence if necessary and reliably had the weapons to back it up. He knew from experience that a lot of the vocal opposition to any government were simply blowhards who didn't have the stomach to do the hard work.

Demyan was thinking of this when he didn't get a response from his first two forum posts. He was now on a gardening website using the alias FertilizerMan. "I'm having a problem with a big rat on my property in the country. Can anyone help me out?"

PestController saw this and alerted his boss, who was a mid-level manager in the currency smuggling division of his cartel. The other divisions were in the standard criminal enterprises of drugs, prostitution, and human smuggling. Black-market currency transactions had become big business with the devaluation of the Venezuelan currency over recent years, and they were also producing counterfeit versions of their cash, which was easier to forge than US dollars. In doing this, they used a lot of different chemicals, including acids, to make the paper money look somewhat used. This was important because of the well-publicized shortage of currency paper in the country. No one had new currency. They also were very familiar with firearms and didn't hesitate to eliminate whoever threatened their business.

The forum was a profitable portal by which the cartel attracted business from other organizations. It seemed the big names knew all the other big names who could get things done outside their sphere of influence, and they valued the low-profile anonymity of the gardening site.

PestController's sole job was to monitor this for the dozen or so code names that represented potential business opportunities. His boss didn't know who FertilizerMan was, but he knew he was important. He had been instructed once to drop everything to accommodate him if he popped up on the site. He was told that the money involved with him was so good that if he didn't respond immediately and lost the business, then his wife and daughter would be used in their trafficking division.

He dictated to his subordinate the response to Demyan.

> **PestController:** We can help with any rats you may have, large or small, one or many, and can start right away. Is that acceptable to you?
>
> **FertilizerMan:** I saw it a while ago, but I've currently lost sight of it. Can I ask you to set up a site close by so that if I see it again, I can shoo it toward you?
>
> **PestController:** Yes, we would be happy to do that.
>
> **FertilizerMan:** We have done business together before. Do you know my property in Nirgua?
>
> **PestController:** It has been a while, but I can look it up and be there shortly. Will that be all right?
>
> **FertilizerMan:** Yes, that would be good. Be sure and bring your biggest rat trap. You will need it.

PestController: We will do that. I have found your address and can be there in two hours with everything we could possibly need.

FertilizerMan: Thank you. Hopefully, I can find him again and herd him there by then. Because this is a much bigger rat than last time, I will double my usual payment.

PestController: Thank you for your confidence in us.

Gyure owned buildings in many parts of the world, both to diversify his income streams and to conduct business confidentially if necessary. This particular building in Nirgua was a four-story parking garage that occupied an entire block in the city center near the hospital. His standing orders were to conduct business at the northeast corner of the third floor of the garage. Payment would be by an obscure cryptocurrency, of course.

Now Demyan had to figure out how to get Khobulin there without the message being intercepted by the Americans. He could tell him that his friends would take him and his car away to the safety of Caracas. But how to get him the info while Khobulin was driving?

Demyan realized that the phone was the weak link. But he needed to communicate explicit instructions to him. Then it dawned on him. He called Khobulin directly.

"Get to an internet café, a library, or any business like a hotel that may have a computer you can use, preferably in a busy place. Then go to our usual plaza." He hoped this would be vague enough to keep any listeners guessing.

Plazas were places where groups of people frequently met—in this case, it was another website that focused on car repairs.

Khobulin found one about twenty minutes later and logged on to the internet.

VintageLover: My old car has a bad rattle. Can anyone help with this?

FixerUpper: I sure can. I can fix anything!

VintageLover: Great? Where are you located?

FixerUpper: I have a mobile unit in Nirgua. Can you make it there? If needed, we can take you and your car to the main shop. Be sure you turn off your vehicle communication box once you get back into it. Sometimes that can cause a nasty rattle.

He gave him the address and trusted that Khobulin would be smart enough to drive around the garage until he found people with a truck that could be a car carrier and turned off his phone.

Khobulin headed toward Nirgua, but he didn't understand the "vehicle communication box." His car was old, and he didn't think it had such technology.

The SigInt tech, meanwhile, back in Washington, DC, was monitoring Khobulin's movements. "Chief," he said, "the mobile signal has stopped moving for the last five minutes, and the UAV is closing on it. We ought to have it in one minute."

"Creech UAV control here. The aircraft that was off our flank came even with us but then dropped back and now is weaving back and forth directly in line with our vector. I'm afraid he's made us."

Anderson and Inaka groaned simultaneously.

The tech watching Caracas Air Base on a different Sentient feed monitor then announced, "And the Su-30 just launched and is heading west at very high speed in the direction of UAV."

————

Sam and Tom Jensen were filling up with gas when a fighter plane screamed overhead, banking south. "That's cool!" Tom said.

"Yeah, I hope they're just joyriding," said Sam. But he had a bad feeling about it.

"It looks like they're heading toward that twin-engine plane ahead of it. I wonder what they did wrong?" Tom said. Then he saw puffs of white smoke trailing behind both wings. "What is that smoke? Are they having problems?"

———

"We've got it," said the technician in DC. "Brown two-door vintage Honda. Got the license plate."

Anderson consulted the satellite feed from San Cristobal. It was a match. "Great, keep it in sight, and don't lose it." Just then, the screen went black.

"Creech here. We've lost all our data from the UAV."

"Did they shoot it down?" Anderson asked.

"That's the most likely scenario."

"Shit!" she said as she slammed her hand on the nearest table. She thought for a moment. "All right then, now we have three big problems. One, we've lost direct visual contact of the car that could lead us to the ultimate architect of the Harbor Day attacks. Two, we have a highly classified piece of technology in tiger country. And three, the Venezuelans know we are there." She paused and then had a new thought. "Where are the Jensens?"

The FBI liaison got on the phone as the NSA people also went to update the plots of their position. Both teams answered her almost simultaneously. "They are just north of the crash site, and only a little farther away is the brown Honda."

"Obviously, they can't track car guy and find and protect the UAV both, so what's the priority?"

Inaka spoke up. "We don't know exactly where the UAV is. It might be scattered across a large area of thick vegetation. We do know exactly where the car is, at least as of a minute ago. Plus, we've got a SEAL team who knows what a UAV looks like, and their mission is to retrieve it, although they are a lot farther away than they wanted to be."

Anderson saw the logic instantly and turned to the technician who was monitoring the UAV feed. "Get as complete a description of the vehicle and any occupants as possible, and get it to the FBI," she said. "They're good at tracking and apprehending people anyway."

What she didn't know was that a big reason the FBI was good at tracking and apprehending people was the sheer volume of people and technology they could bring to bear on any target. With the exception of Venezuela. Their volume in Venezuela was exactly one agent and a helper of unknown capability. They would have to try to get that one agent the benefit of as much technology as they could muster from such a long distance.

———

"Yes, sir, copy that," said Sam into the satellite phone. He turned to Tom and said, "Write this down," and gave him the license plate number. "We are looking for an old brown two-door Honda on Highway 7 to Barquisimeto. It was last seen stopped outside a business in the town of Quibor. We assume he's trying to get to Caracas, but he could stop anywhere along the way."

Tom quickly checked the map on his phone. "Okay, that's good. Our road intersects with that highway east of Quibor, about five miles away. We are currently about the same distance from that highway intersection."

"Great," said Sam. "We need to hoof it to get there before him. Then we'll fake some car trouble and wait for him. Hopefully, he won't be ahead of us, or it's going to be a really sucky day."

Ten minutes later, they were stopped on the side of Highway 7, with Sam seeming to be looking under the hood but, in reality, looking at the oncoming traffic. Tom was on the outside shoulder of the car doing the same thing while looking into the open trunk. "I think I see it coming over that hill behind us," Sam said loudly over the traffic noise.

"Yep, I got it," replied Tom.

"Okay, let's wait for him to get around that next curve. Then we'll close up and head after him. We don't want any extra movement on our part to scare him."

Thirty seconds later, they closed the doors as Sam accelerated into the driving lane. Once they rounded the curve, they saw the brown Honda about a quarter mile away. Sam slowly closed the distance to keep him in sight easily but far enough back not to arouse his attention.

"Now what?" Tom asked.

———

Khobulin was focused on the address in the town of Nirgua that he was rapidly approaching. He weaved his way into the heart of the city and found the hospital and then the parking garage. He entered it without seeing the rental car carrying two men around the corner that he'd just come from. He slowly snaked his way through the lanes between the parked cars, starting on the ground level. When he didn't see anything, he went up to the second level and repeated the pattern; then he did the third. The spaces were mostly occupied, but not completely, and at the far end of the last corner, he saw a car carrier with two people standing outside it smoking cigarettes.

"Are you from the car repair place?" Khobulin asked.

"Sí, señor, are you the one with the bad rattle?"

"Yes, I'm glad you're here. I need some help, please."

"Unfortunately, we didn't bring the right tools for that. We'll have to get you and the car to the main shop."

"Fine with me," said Khobulin. He felt better being undercover in the parking garage, protected from overlying satellites or drones. But he still wanted to get to better safety. "Let's get going."

The two men maneuvered the ramp of the car carrier to the ground while Khobulin lined up the car to drive up it. They paid no attention to the vehicle with two men slowly driving past them.

"Damn, did you see the muscles on the guys with the truck?" Tom asked after they passed the trio.

"Sure did, but I also noticed both of their noses were crooked, and one had cauliflower ears. They are seasoned fighters. That complicates things."

Sam thought for another moment. He and his nephew had taken care of three guys, more or less, but those men didn't make a living foisting violence on others. And the Jensens had the benefit of surprise. And they had lost one target in the process, although they traced his contact to here. They didn't have a chance against three skilled operators whose guard was up.

The only way to deal with this was to follow them or find out where they were going. Both options had to place them closer to the bad guys than felt safe.

Sam pulled out of the garage, turned right, and fortunately found a nearby empty spot at the curb, where he pulled in. A few minutes later, the car carrier exited the building with a black tarp over the car in the back. Three men were in the cab of the truck, and the one closest to the passenger window had a deformed ear.

"Well, at least this will be easier to follow for a while." He got on the satellite phone once they were about four cars back from the carrier and relayed the new information to Washington. He maintained a healthy distance from the truck as it slowly made its way out of town, headed toward Caracas.

FOURTEEN

JOE PARK WAS KNOCKING ON DOORS of Korean businesses and restaurants all along Highway 99 north of Seattle, in Shoreline. This was the biggest of the three main areas where newly arrived Koreans tended to settle. He figured that, most likely, a new guy would want to try to make his life easier by going where others spoke his language, so Joe visited and left photos of the man he was looking for—the drone operator from Puget Sound—with the Korean convenience stores, restaurants, and cleaners.

He also scanned as many of the men on the sidewalks as he could while he was doing this, but frankly, a lot looked outwardly like his suspect, so he was hoping for another break like the drone store kid who'd remembered the suspect as a customer.

His feet were killing him late in the day when he stepped into an old but clean Korean restaurant next to an older and less clean apartment complex. He gave the photo and his spiel to the woman behind the cashier's desk.

"Oh, yeah, I know this guy. He was in here just the other day."

"How do you know it was him?"

"It was the same face, same coat, everything."

"Was there anything special you remember about him?"

"Yeah, he was a bad tipper."

Joe's heart sank a little. It's not uncommon for people to call the police on minor infractions or insults just to get even.

"Okay, anything else?"

"He had a North Korean accent."

"North Korean? Are you sure?"

She looked at him like he was an idiot. "My parents defected from there twenty-five years ago, then got shipped here to safety. They have the same accent."

"Do you know where I might find him now?"

"No, but he was a walk-in, no car, so he might be local."

Joe stepped out to call his SAC, and two hours later, there were twenty FBI agents and twenty more Shoreline PD officers knocking on doors of the nearest apartment complex, with the Northwest Regional Hostage Rescue Team setting up out of sight two blocks away in case they were needed. While they weren't necessarily expecting a hostage situation to be present, the HRT was well-trained in handling multiple types of lethal force incidents.

Joe was paired with a young Shoreline police officer who looked like he'd just finished the academy. He had knocked on every door of the floor he was assigned except the last two. It was obvious to any casual observer that the authorities were looking for someone. Word traveled fast in such a situation, so as he and his new partner were showing the lady at the end of the hall the picture of the suspect, the door opposite them jerked open, and a figure bounded out and through the adjacent fire escape door to squirt down the stairs.

Joe shot a questioning look at his partner that said, *Why weren't you watching the hallway? That's your job!* He then motioned with his finger and pointed to the now-closing door in the universal sign of "Go get him!"

His partner took off like a gazelle. Joe was fit at age thirty-four, but he was no gazelle. He radioed Incident Command with the situation.

———

"Things just got worse," said the FBI liaison at the NSA. He relayed the new information from Venezuela about the brown Honda now being transported via a car carrier, along with two beefy fighters, to Nancy Anderson's crew.

"Got it," said the technician on the satellite feed. "At least a tow truck is a bigger target than the little car."

"What other assets do we have that can help us track that vehicle?" asked Anderson.

"We only have the satellites we're using or poaching the data from," one of the technicians responded.

Another tech spoke up. "We also still have the phone signal that we were tracking before, so it's definitely the guy we're looking for."

That was a rare stroke of luck, thought Anderson. "What else do we know about Khobulin?"

"All we know is his employment in the Uzbeki Intelligence service. We've been running down the numbers in his cell phone history, and there is one that continues to be 'ghosted,' as it were. We are still trying to find its provenance, but whoever set it up is very, very good. Interestingly, he received a call from the same number during this trip."

"That's got to be the higher-up we're looking for," replied Inaka. "Keep working on identifying that contact. Use all resources necessary. I'll make sure you get them. And until we get that info, we need to do everything possible to keep this guy alive." He then turned to the FBI liaison. "Tell your guys not to kill anybody in that truck. They need to be captured."

The FBI liaison paled. He knew how difficult it would be for one agent and an untrained civilian to capture three battle-tested bad guys. "With all due respect, we need to get these guys help to carry out that mission. One and a half against three is terrible odds, and they are probably going into a location where the targets have lots of backup."

Inaka spoke up. "The SEAL team in the country is too far away. Is there another one on that sub? And, for that matter, can we get another drone launched that might help surveil the truck?"

The DOD liaison got on his phone, and a few minutes later, he answered that question. "The drone is a no-go. The bosses don't know how they located the first one, and they don't want another one put in harm's way. As for human help, yes, there is another team on that sub, and they are looking for a suitable place they can infiltrate now. The absolute earliest they can try to get someone there is four hours, assuming it's

near Caracas. But that whole area is very populated, so it will be difficult
to get into the country without being seen, even at night."

———

Far down the next block, the tow truck turned into what appeared to be
a private driveway. When the Jensens got to it after the light changed,
they saw nothing but a closed solid gate. On either side was an opaque
eight-foot-high fence that was free of any handholds, topped by razor
wire, and backed by what looked to be impenetrable tall vegetation. It
seemed to go on forever. In fact, when they began circling the block, they
noticed that there were discreetly placed cameras every hundred yards
or so, and there was a maze of streets that dead-ended into the fence.
It was like the streetside entrance was the tip of the iceberg, and they
couldn't identify exactly how big it was.

"Whoever this is, they definitely like their privacy," Sam said to himself
as he lifted the satellite radio. "Do you guys have eyes on this property?"

"Yes, we are looking at it now via satellite," replied the DOJ liaison.
One of the NSA techs began to research the data associated with the
property to help determine the size, owner, infrastructure, etc. Another
simply mapped the area enclosed by the fence.

"I've got it measuring roughly twelve acres inside that fence. There
are a lot of big trees there, and I can see four buildings for sure, but there
may be many more hidden by the trees or situated underground," said
the second tech. "I can see the main entrance on the south side, and it
looks like another one on the north side is a secondary type of access.
In addition, multiple dead-end streets lead up to the fence all around the
property, and they are full of structures, either residential or commercial buildings."

"Well, shit," said Anderson. "We really need to see what's going on in
there. Do they see any other way in, maybe over or through the fence?"

The liaison relayed that to Sam, who explained the fence's impervi-
ousness and the intensive monitoring of the property line.

"I have an idea," said Tom. "I still have my drone. It's pretty quiet,
and once I get it launched, I may be able to pick a way through or over

the vegetation to get inside the wire. I will have real-time video feedback here on my controller. I can look all around, but I might not know what I'm seeing."

Sam relayed that to the NSA, and they responded enthusiastically. "We can tap into that real-time feed and analyze it here, which may help you guys on the ground."

Sam pulled over in one of the dead ends near the fence while Tom retrieved his backpack and dug out the drone case. It took a minute or two to set it up and make sure it was functioning. They made sure they were out of the line of sight of the video cameras on the fence and then launched it. It was surprisingly quiet, difficult to hear more than ten to fifteen yards away. Tom started clockwise around the property, and several hundred yards later, he found a gap in the trees. He maneuvered the drone through the opening, careful to stay several feet above the level of the cameras, which were all angled downward to keep the entire fence in view.

―――

Gellert Demyan sat at the lone table in the large warehouse in the heavily wooded property outside Caracas. It was extremely dangerous for him to have flown to Caracas from Cuba, where he had been establishing another network, but he felt it was the best way to make sure that Khobulin didn't get compromised.

The tow truck with the three men and the car had driven straight into the warehouse. Khobulin was directed to the table. Demyan knew what he wanted to do with Khobulin, but dealing with the car would be trickier. First, though, he needed all the information he could get from the Uzbeki to make sure there were no other loose ends that needed to be dealt with.

Khobulin was initially relieved when he entered the warehouse with his new contacts. Once he saw the darkened face of Gellert Demyan, though, he became uneasy. The more he looked around at the warehouse and the predatory stares of the other men, the more apprehensive he became and the more he started to look for a way out if things went sideways. He quickly decided he would have to fight his way out of the building, but he was well-trained and developed a plan as he talked to Demyan.

"Where did you dump the mobile phone?" Demyan asked Khobulin.

"I didn't. It is right here," Khobulin said as he pulled it out of his pocket.

Demyan's face reddened. "I told you to get rid of it in the message on the forum! You know the Americans have probably traced us here!"

Khobulin sensed it was time to act and popped out of his chair while simultaneously lifting the table into Demyan's face, knocking him backward off his chair. It also caught the armed cartel member coming to Demyan's side, knocking his short-barreled rifle out of his hands onto the floor. Khobulin got to the rifle first, shot the man twice in the upper chest, and then spun to engage other targets as he sprinted for the nearest door.

———

Sam and Tom Jensen were watching the feed from the drone as it was circling the building when they saw a door fly open, and a man ran out armed with a short rifle. He ran in a zig-zag pattern, apparently because he was being shot at from inside the building. The Americans could hear the shots from their vantage point in their rental car. Sam realized this could be a positive development for them. If they could capture this guy, it might give them valuable intel on the occupants and contacts of those on the property.

"Which way is he going relative to us, Tom?"

"We are west of the property, and he turned to go north, so he is going to our left."

Sam decided that if the fence was strong enough to keep people out, it was also strong enough to keep them in. To the north lay the secondary exit. Khobulin had instinctively chosen to head opposite the heavily armed entrance but didn't know the north access point was only lightly defended.

Sam started the car and told Tom, "Keep the guy in sight but far enough behind or to the side that he can't hear the drone. I'm going to that north exit the NSA people told us about. That's his only way out. Keep me updated with his progress."

"Roger that!" Tom was enjoying the feeling of the sudden increased pace of the action.

Sam explained the details of his plan as their car screamed up the north road to the small exit gate. "He's got a rifle, and he's jumpy and primed to use it at the first inkling of trouble. So we've got to take him by surprise and get the rifle from him quickly." Sam skidded to a stop as Tom gave him the update on where the runner was. Then they jumped out of the car and took up positions on either side of the gate.

They heard a few bursts of rifle fire on the other side of the fence as Khobulin, on the opposite side, took out the three men just inside. The gate flew open, and Sam quickly grabbed the rifle at the barrel to better control the direction it would be pointing. Tom came from the other side simultaneously and instinctively grabbed the midportion of the rifle to cover the ejection port. Khobulin fired one round into the building across the street, but Tom's hand over the ejection port prevented the cartridge from ejecting free, and it clogged the chamber, causing the gun to jam. It was now useless, and it would take even an experienced shooter a minute or two to clear it.

Sam kept hold of the barrel while Tom released his grip and pivoted to get behind Khobulin. He reached around the man's throat with his left arm while he hit his jaw with his right fist to get his larynx perfectly positioned in the crook of his elbow and then applied the rear naked choke hold. Once his hands were in a perfect position, Tom pushed the man's head forward and took a deep breath. He only held it for about ten seconds, and the man went limp and collapsed.

Sam quickly applied zip ties to Khobulin's wrists and ankles and then zip-tied them together so that he was folded outward, and the two Americans bundled him into the back seat of their rental car, lying on his side, and then drove off. They left the rifle on the sidewalk.

The authorities might be able to get their fingerprints off the rifle, but they planned to be long gone by then.

FIFTEEN

IVAN POPOV FOUND O'MALLEY, and they were now together in Chuck Haggard's office at the NYPD Human Trafficking Unit.

"Tell us everything you know so far," said Haggard to Popov.

Popov reiterated the background he had already relayed to Haggard for O'Malley's benefit. "We traced their communications as far back as possible. The earliest we could find was about two years ago. 'Andrei Chikatilo' contacted Upshaw, who was using a pseudonym on the dark web that was not very creative, so we easily figured out who he was and what organization he was with. 'Chikatilo' was looking for a like-minded person who could help with a problem. They used oblique references at the time, but now appear in retrospect to be describing the sinking of the ships in the New York/New Jersey port."

Haggard and O'Malley both sat forward in their seats.

"It also appears that they had a face-to-face meeting somewhere in the US about eighteen months ago."

Haggard asked, "Who else knows about this?"

"Just us three for now."

Haggard instantly knew that this could be a huge break in the case to find those responsible for killing his wife—and all those other passengers on the cruise ship the day of the massive explosion. He and his kids were still grappling with the grief and enormous feeling of loss. His kids were struggling in school and getting into more conflicts there and at home. He knew their "acting out" was a sign of depression that he felt helpless to fix. He missed Theresa desperately. The huge hole in his heart pained him so much that he had trouble focusing on many tasks. That difficulty just disappeared with Popov's information. His mind snapped to focus like a laser to catch this man. "Where is Upshaw now?"

Popov replied, "Not surprisingly, he has gone dark since O'Malley here killed a couple of his guys."

A plan formed in Haggard's head. He punched a button on his desk phone. "Rufus, get in here, please."

Thirty seconds later, Rufus Johnson came in. "Yessir?"

Haggard briefed him. When he was done, he said, "So we have two people we need to find. We know the name of one—Jack Upshaw. The other uses the pseudonym of Andrei Chikatilo, thought to be in Russia. We need to find them both as quickly as possible. I want five of your best people detailed to each one of them. Find them now."

"On it." Johnson turned and left.

———

Joe Park caught up with his young partner, who had tackled the squirter around the back corner from the building they had run out of in Shoreline, north of Seattle. All three of them were out of breath. His partner had the man's legs, and Joe landed his knee on the man's back, grabbed his wrists, and placed handcuffs on him. The suspect continued to struggle for about another minute before he tired. When they finally lifted him upright, he saw Joe; a look of confusion and then alarm crossed his face.

"Why did you run from us?" Joe asked. He was rewarded with silence. "Do you speak English?" No answer. He switched to Korean and asked again. The man's eyes twitched almost imperceptibly, but he still didn't speak.

"All right, let's get him down to the station so we can do this formally," said Joe. His partner then radioed his command to apprise them of the situation and to dispatch a vehicle to their location to transport the man downtown. Meanwhile, Joe used his cell to call his SAC.

"Chief, I think he's Korean, maybe North Korean."

"What makes you think that?"

"He never said a word, but he looked confused and then scared when he saw me. He didn't respond at all to English, but when I spoke to him in Korean, he gave away a tell that made me think he understood. Regardless, he won't be cooperative. I'm going to take his picture on my phone now and run it to the lady at the restaurant to see if she will confirm it's the same guy she was thinking about. Then I need the contact info of that couple from Fort Casey, who saw the guy on their GoPro camera the day of the attacks, to see if they can identify him as well."

"Great," replied the SAC, "I'll get that for you. In the meantime, I'll bump this up and get the techies involved to try to find out who this guy is."

———

Agent Stefano Alvarez was supervising the collection of evidence from the wreckage of the *Leviathan*, the Defender-class Coast Guard escort, and the boat that crashed into and sank the mammoth cruise ship at PortMiami. The bodies were still being recovered from the cruise ship, but the authorities were dragging the bed of the channel for hundreds of yards around it. They were transporting what wreckage they could find to Cruise Terminal G for evaluation and examination.

It was a tedious task. The crews on the search boats first had to identify an object using sonar, map the GPS coordinates, retrieve it, label it, and then transport it to the collection site. Because they wanted information as quickly as possible, they had to make a trip to shore after each "find." They were lucky enough to have three search boats running almost twenty-four hours a day, changing out crews every twelve hours. But some locations only had one search boat available, which made the collection of evidence painfully slow.

The cruise terminal housed marine engineers, marine architects, representatives from the manufacturers of the two known boats, forensic metallurgic technicians, and representatives from the cruise line and Coast Guard to help identify any corporate or personal property. Drone manufacturer representatives were also invited, but they were all still stuck in China for so-called logistic reasons. The National Transportation

Safety Board had experience investigating airplane crashes, so they took overall control of the process.

When an item came to the intake area of the terminal, it was logged into the master database along with its location data, photographed from six different angles, and then sent to the marine architects and engineers to try first to identify whether it came from one of the subject boats. If it looked like it did, it was sent to the larger room if it was thought to have come from the *Leviathan* and the smaller room if it was thought to have come from the Defender. All others went to a third room for additional examination. Computer technicians mapped out the locations of the pieces of metal found on the channel bed, and as their provenance became known, they were given a color—red for Coast Guard, blue for *Leviathan,* and green for others.

Gradually a picture began to emerge on the computer of which pieces of debris from the various vessels landed where. A big problem was the other green evidence. It was hoped that the majority of the evidence not positively identified as belonging to the two known vessels would be from the targeting boat. A lot of debris had collected on the channel bed over the years, so it took extra time to try to sort that out. In all these rooms, the marine engineers and architects tried to put the pieces back together as much as possible to get a visual picture of the boats at the moment of impact.

Agent Alvarez was usually in the command office with the other senior people assimilating and trying to interpret the evidence coming in. He was working eighteen-hour days and would periodically retreat to an unused office with a couch to put his feet up and clear his head, usually with his eyes closed.

There was a rap on the door frame. It was the NTSB representative. "Agent Alvarez, we may have found something."

He was instantly on his feet. "What do you have?"

The NTSB man handed him a piece of metal wrapped in plastic. Alvarez raised his upturned palms in confusion.

"This piece of debris was found today about two hundred yards directly perpendicular from the impact site on the *Leviathan.*"

"And?"

"It's part of a transom bracket for a 300-horsepower Yamaha outboard motor."

Alvarez's eyes widened. He looked at the debris. It was clear it had been violently deformed. "How do you know?"

"That small metal plate that is secured to it has the model number and the serial number on it."

"Okay, could it be from the Coastie?"

"I checked with their guy. They only use 225-horsepower engines on their Defenders."

Alvarez laid the debris on the desk and called his SAC. "I've got some good news . . ."

After he hung up with his boss, he called Yamaha and had them look up the sales info for that engine. They'd sold it to Invincible Boat Company in Opa-locka, Florida. He called them next and asked to speak with the CEO, who picked up immediately.

Alvarez explained his situation and asked if they could connect the serial number of a Yamaha engine to a particular boat and then trace the provenance of that boat.

"Yes, we can do that. But if the subsequent owner or owners change out the engine later, then all bets are off."

"I understand. But if you can get me the info that you have, we can start with that."

"Sure, I'll call you back within the hour."

Fifteen minutes later, Alvarez's phone rang. "It turns out this was added to our thirty-three-foot Open Fisherman model we sold from the factory in Opa-locka directly to a company called Super SportFishing in Miami five years ago. We don't have records of any contact with subsequent owners if there are any."

"That's a great start," Alvarez said. "Thank you very much, sir."

Alvarez was invigorated now. He pounded his fist on the desk and called Super SportFishing. There was no answer. He left a voice mail and then looked up the address, grabbed his windbreaker, and ran to his car.

SIXTEEN

HAGGARD AND O'MALLEY WERE SITTING in Chuck's office in One Police Plaza discussing plans for what they'd do when their team located one of the suspects when Rufus came in.

"We just got a ping on Upshaw."

"Tell me."

"We were scouring the credit card companies and found a Jack Upshaw bought some gas at a convenience store in Arkansas an hour ago. We traced that number, and there has been no other activity on that card over the last month. Prior to that was typical daily living stuff all around Bayonne, New Jersey."

O'Malley asked, "Does he have any record of going to that part of the country before? Any phone calls to that area? Any known family there?"

"Not that we've found, sir," replied Johnson.

Haggard asked, "What about his phone records? Has he been in communication with anyone out of the country?"

"We are looking at that also. Nothing obvious yet, but we're still looking. Also, still nothing on the dark web site that he used with the 'Chikatilo' guy."

O'Malley mused, "Could he be going to Mexico by car?" The others looked at him.

"That makes a lot of sense," said Haggard. "We need to cut him off. Paul, let your folks know what's going on and that we need one of their jets to try to pre-position us, where he is most likely to be in about six

hours. Since you have laid eyes on him, we need you to be there to help
identify him. Then meet me back here so we can go to the airport. Great
work, Rufus." Haggard shook Johnson's hand with the vise-like grip he
was known for, a steely determination in his eye.

Haggard called up a US map on his computer. He mapped out the
general direction from New Jersey to Arkansas. He knew it was about
a three-hour flight to Texas. He figured that would be the most likely
route to Mexico. He wanted to have a cushion of time in case of flight
delays.

When O'Malley returned from his phone call, they went to the
armory first. "Get whatever you think we'll need. Thank God we won't
have to worry about TSA. Or Texas. We are going to San Antonio."

Together they each got a small AR pistol, a carbine-length rifle, and
six loaded magazines for each. They both were already carrying their
sidearms with extra mags, so they also added four extra magazines for
each of them and loaded them all into transport bags.

"It just so happens there is a Hostage Rescue Team here in the city.
They will meet us at the airport," said O'Malley.

"Great," said Haggard. He thought he could handle Upshaw by
himself, but he wouldn't turn down the help of a bunch of highly trained
friends with a lot of firepower.

———

Park was now at the Seattle police station watching the techs process
their prisoner. They not only photographed and fingerprinted him but
also took retinal scans and a DNA sample from a swab inside the suspect's cheek. Park then entered the interview room, sat opposite him,
and asked him in Korean, "How is your family?"

The prisoner looked at him in a way Park thought was too quick.
"You know it's only a matter of time before we find out exactly who you
are. We are the best in the world at that. Then we will find your family. Their names, ages . . ." He paused for dramatic effect. "Locations."
The prisoner started to sweat above his upper lip. It was an autonomic
response he could not control.

Park knew he could get to this guy.

"You know we also have people in the DPRK," Park went on. "People that look and talk just like you. There are probably some even in your neighborhood." He was playing on his subject's inherent paranoia. Everyone in North Korea was paranoid. Operatives working undercover overseas were even more so.

"Now you can play the quiet game as long as you like. But also know that the longer it takes to find your family, the harder it will be for them." The sweating increased.

"On the other hand, if you start talking now, we will keep an eye out for them. Try to keep the bad guys away from them." He stood up to leave.

"Wait," replied the prisoner.

———

Agent Alvarez pulled up to the address of the Super SportFishing company at the marina in Coral Gables, just south of Miami. As he exited the car, he looked around for anything suspicious. It all looked like regular marina activity. He fixed his gaze on the door. The inside was dark. He pulled on the door, but it was locked. The business hours sign said they should be open, but clearly weren't. He called the number on the sign but got the same voice mail message he'd gotten earlier. He was starting to think he was onto something now. He called his SAC, who already had his people looking for more information about the owner. He gave the home address to Alvarez while starting the process for an emergency search warrant for the business and organizing a team to go through it.

An hour later, Alvarez was back at the shop after finding the house locked up as tight as the business office. The FBI found that the owner was divorced and there were no kids. The SAC in the Miami Field Office insisted they go by the book. He didn't want anyone getting off on a technicality. Alvarez understood, knowing the Bureau had been playing too loose with the rules in recent years. So he waited with the rest of the crew outside the office. Finally, he got the call from his SAC saying the warrant had been signed.

Alvarez gave the go-ahead to the team to begin entry. They had already notified the Coral Gables police, so they wouldn't be surprised if someone called in about a break-in in progress, which is what this was.

It was a simple lock to pick, and the team entered quickly and fanned out across the office. The place consisted of only three rooms—the front with a counter, telephone, computer, calendar, and display rack with informational pamphlets and branded merchandise; a back office with a desk, computer, and file cabinet; and a smaller side room with fishing gear.

Alvarez saw the calendar and went immediately to it. The last entry was April 14, labeled *Ian Ndobo—4 hrs*. He made another call.

"The only Ian Ndobo we have around here is in El Portal," said the voice at the Field Office, who gave him the address.

"Give this info to the SAC and have him get a search warrant there, too. I'm on the way." Alvarez grabbed two of his team from the office, and together they ran out the door.

———

Sam and Tom were en route to the center of Caracas. Tom was watching their prisoner in the back seat while Sam headed northeastward toward the water. He got on the satellite phone to relay their situation, location, and heading as best he knew.

"Roger that, stand by one," came the reply from the comms officer at NSA, where the Venezuela operation was being coordinated. The officer then relayed the info to the joint group managing it. The Defense liaison told the rest about the SEAL team already on the ground and the one that had recently left the sub by Shallow Water Combat Submersible. "We can redirect the incoming team to wherever would be the most advantageous point on the coast, pick them up, and bring them back to the sub."

They all looked at the map and realized that extraction by sub would be a much faster route to safety than driving to a neighboring country. "How big is that SWCS? Can they all fit in it?" asked the FBI liaison.

"It will carry six SEALs, including the driver," said the DOD liaison.

"It's fully loaded because we didn't know what we would be needing. That means we'll have to offload three guys. It won't be a problem. That's what they do. We'll get them back later."

They all agreed and then settled on a location west of Caracas, an area dotted by small towns, with long stretches of beaches and coves in between. "Article," said the comms officer, using the call sign they came up with via the random word generator. "Here is your new destination." He gave them the name of the nearest town, directions, and geographic coordinates, hoping they could figure it out. They were hamstrung somewhat by having to use common names, which would be easy for another party to figure out if they could break the encryption system they were using. "We will extract you from there."

Khobulin appeared to be comatose in the back seat, but he was listening to the whole conversation. He was nervous because he was in the company of Americans, and they would show no mercy in getting the information out of his head. On the other hand, he felt safer than he did in the warehouse they'd just taken him from.

"Okay," said Tom, who was looking at the map. "Puerto Cabello is west of here. Then it looks like they are directing us to a pretty undeveloped area within a cove just east of there. It looks like there is a small road that will take us there." He hoped there was a road there, anyway. He knew from experience that roads on a map in Latin America were frequently just a suggestion. "Turn left at the next intersection."

SEVENTEEN

HAGGARD, O'MALLEY, AND THE FBI Hostage Rescue Team landed at Kelly Field in San Antonio. They were unloading their gear into a pair of government-issue Suburbans when a government sedan drove up, and a uniformed man exited the driver's seat.

"Which one of you is Chuck Haggard?" asked the newcomer.

Haggard raised his free hand, the one that was not carrying the long gun bag, and squinted at the man.

"I'm Captain Rogers, the XO of the base commander here. The general wants you to know he is aware of your current mission and offers you his full support as well as any personnel or equipment, including air assets, that you may need."

"Thank you, Captain. Right now, we need a place to park and update our information and set up plans for going forward with this. Do you have a couple of vacant rooms where we can do that?"

"Of course, sir. Follow me."

Five minutes later, they entered a low-slung building at the end of the flight line, and Captain Rogers led them to the last two rooms at the end of the first-floor hall.

Within an hour, they had set up their makeshift armory, computers, whiteboards, phones, and radios in one room and personal gear in the next. They would figure out sleeping arrangements later.

Haggard then phoned Rufus to see if Upshaw had left any more crumbs. "We got the security cam feed from the convenience store, and it looks like the guy is in a white Dodge Durango—an older model. He doesn't have one registered to him, so it's probably either borrowed or stolen. We don't have license plates on it because the camera angle and quality were poor, but we are plugged into the highway departments of Arkansas, Oklahoma, and Texas to see if we can find him on their highway cams. I've diverted half a dozen more people to help with this."

"Great. And?"

"We are pretty sure we've tracked him to south of Dallas now on Interstate 35."

Haggard checked the map. "Well, that makes sense. It is the straightest shot to the border if he's going there. And it comes straight through San Antonio. Great work. Keep me updated, please."

Haggard turned to his team and relayed the information. "I'd rather not confront him in a major urban area, though, and we don't know where he might divert, so I think we ought to head north and intercept him in a rural area if possible."

As the team was heading north, Haggard learned that his team had identified twelve white Dodge Durangos in the general area, which meant it was going to be tough to locate the one Upshaw was driving. He turned to O'Malley. "We are going to need more resources. Can you talk to your people to notify and coordinate with all the local law enforcement agencies between there and here to look for any white Durangos? I don't want to stop them yet, but if they can stage at multiple points along the way, follow one, get the license plate to run through the system, and rule out ones that are obvious locals, we can hopefully narrow things down."

"Roger that," replied O'Malley. He relayed the request to his headquarters, along with the description of Upshaw that officers could use. An obvious potential problem was if Upshaw ditched this vehicle for a different one or started taking back roads. They were hoping he was the anxious amateur they thought he was and would be focused on getting to safety as quickly as possible.

Ninety minutes later, Rufus called Haggard. "Jack Upshaw just bought some gas with his known credit card in Jarrell, Texas, at a convenience store on I-35."

"Copy that. Any video at the store?"

"Yes, both inside and outside the store. It's him. And he is in a white Dodge Durango."

"Great work, Rufus. Any highway cameras near that area?"

"The nearest one is about twenty miles south of there. We are watching it like a hawk."

Haggard replied, "Perfect. We will coordinate from here. Keep me posted."

"Roger that, boss."

Finally, Haggard could sense he was getting closer to finding the thread that would lead him to his wife's killer. He noticed he was breathing harder and forced himself to combat breathe—to calm himself down so he could think better. He inhaled slowly for a count of six seconds, held his breath for another six, exhaled slowly for six seconds, and then paused another six seconds with his lungs empty.

They were north of Austin now, and O'Malley then relayed the new information to his contacts, who broadcast them to the relevant nearby agencies. Five minutes later, they started seeing multiple law enforcement vehicles of all stripes on the interstate, northward and southward. O'Malley also asked for any helicopter assistance available and was told there were already two birds in the air headed their way.

Ten minutes later, they were notified that a white Durango with New Jersey plates driven by a white male who appeared to be the lone occupant was going south, entering Pflugerville, just north of Austin.

"That's him. Detail the one who identified him to keep him in sight, and have the LEOs behind him discreetly slow down and then block the traffic behind him. Also, have them start blocking entrance ramps going south from there. He is considered armed and dangerous, so we need to minimize exposure to the regular public. We are just entering Pflugerville from the south, so we will turn around and head in the same direction for the intercept. We will be the lead for stopping him."

———

Upshaw was focused on getting as far south as fast as possible without drawing attention to himself, so he didn't see the traffic behind him

thinning out. He was starting to see entrance ramps to the highway
being blocked by police cars. Then he noticed that instead of increasing traffic going into Austin, there were fewer vehicles on the road. He
started getting nervous and then realized that the sheriff's SUV that was
behind him by a quarter mile was matching his speed. He gripped the
steering wheel harder as he began looking for a way off the highway.

A government SUV was going slow in the right lane, so he switched
to the left and started to pass it. Just then, he noticed another one in
front that suddenly switched to the left lane and started going slower
than the one in the right lane. He swore and changed again to the right
lane as the first one drifted forward. The SUVs began slowing, and he
then noticed the sheriff's vehicle behind him. He realized he was being
boxed in.

As quickly as a plan formed in his head, he slammed on the brakes.
The SUVs in front and to the side kept going while the vehicle behind
him reflexively braked also. He was able to squeeze through the opening left by the other two and accelerated to where he was just in front
of the one in the middle lane. He swerved sharply to the right and
rammed the adjacent vehicle, which then veered off into the other SUV
to its right, which then ran off the road.

Good, he thought, *only two more to deal with*. He pushed the gas
pedal to the floor.

———

Haggard was sitting in the passenger seat of the SUV that had gotten
rammed by Upshaw and was royally pissed. O'Malley was in the left
rear passenger seat and got a good look at the driver. "That's him, no
doubt."

O'Malley started working the radios. "I need spike strips and bar-
ricades at all the exit ramps going south." *We'll chase him till he runs
out of gas*, he thought. *Unfortunately, he just filled up, so we may run
out first.*

Haggard didn't want to kill Upshaw, which was possible if they did
a PIT maneuver on him, and he rolled and was ejected from the vehicle.

He got back on the radio. "We are at mile marker 238, heading south-bound. We need spike strips crossing the entire highway by mile marker 230." They were in the middle of Austin now, and he wanted him stopped on the outskirts of town, if possible, where it was less congested.

"Roger that, sir. Vectoring officers there now," replied the dispatcher.

"All right, guys," he announced to the rest of the people in his SUV, three of whom were HRT. "We need him alive and able to talk, so no lethal force unless he uses it on you first."

"Roger that, sir," they all answered.

Suddenly, Upshaw swerved right, between two exits, at a high rate of speed. He bounced down the embankment, hit a depression, and rolled his Durango multiple times before coming to a rest on its roof.

Haggard's driver slowed to keep pace with Upshaw, finally stopping when Upshaw's car stopped. They bolted out of the SUV and raced to the Durango, where they found him unconscious, lying on the ceiling of his vehicle.

The helicopter circling overhead saw the events unfold and called for EMS while the team on the ground surrounded and secured the scene. One officer bent down and crawled inside to look for weapons and to make sure he was breathing, which he was.

EIGHTEEN

AGENT STEFANO ALVAREZ'S CELL PHONE rang as he pulled up to Ian Ndobo's house in El Portal. "We have the search warrant. Again, do everything by the book," said his SAC at the Miami Field Office.

"Roger that, sir."

He went to the front door as his teammates fanned to the left and right of the house to both provide overwatch and, they hoped, get eyes on anyone trying to leave out the back. It was theoretically possible for someone to go straight back out the back door, but there was only an intracoastal canal at that point, so it would be unlikely for anyone to get far unless they had a boat docked and ready to go.

Alvarez knocked, announced his presence, and got no response. He peered in the adjacent windows, noticed the lights were off, and no one seemed home. He gestured to his teammate, who again picked the lock, and they entered with guns drawn, again announcing their presence.

He had previously gotten information that Ndobo had no family, but that didn't mean he had no friends living with him, so the team carefully searched every room in the house for other people before looking for additional information regarding Ian Ndobo.

They then photographed the rooms, systematically searched for any items that might help them trace his existence, and found a computer with a book next to it in a bedroom used as an office. They put these and a cell phone from the other room into the entryway prior to the evidence collection team arriving. The rest of the house was quite spartan, but they went through all the drawers, closets, linens, and clothing for hidden items. They even turned over the mattresses, searched under the beds, and found nothing else. The dock outside likewise was empty, and they did not find any obvious incriminating items. They would have to wait for the forensics team to search for additional evidence.

———

Upshaw had been knocked unconscious by the vehicle rolling, but only for a few seconds. When he realized the agents were coming for him and he couldn't quickly escape, he decided to play possum. He undid his seat belt once he realized he had no other injuries and let himself fall to the ceiling, arranging to place his head and one leg at a strange angle. He was hoping the agents wouldn't notice the gun inside his waistband behind his belt buckle.

EMS came and dragged him out of the overturned Durango, placed him in a cervical collar and on a backboard, and loaded him into the back of the ambulance for transport.

This might actually work, Upshaw thought.

The nearby hospital had a trauma team waiting for him. Once he arrived, they jumped into their routine of starting IV lines and cutting his clothes off. He used that opportunity to "wake up." As he suddenly jerked all his extremities, the surrounding staff jumped back in surprise. He instantly lifted his shirt with his left hand and reached into his waistband with his right.

Dr. John Jensen was running the resuscitation from his usual location at the foot of the stretcher. He immediately recognized the maneuver since he had done it thousands of times. He instinctively stepped to the right side of the bed by Upshaw's waist and used both hands to grab Upshaw's hand as it was coming out of his waistband. The patient did indeed have a 9mm pistol.

Jensen covered the ejection port with his left hand and the muzzle with his right to wrest the gun away from the man by turning it to the wall opposite him.

But Upshaw pulled the trigger, which was deafening in that enclosed room, and the round went into the opposite wall.

Jensen knew the gun was now inoperable since the brass case jammed in the chamber. Jensen felt Upshaw pull the trigger a couple more times before realizing it was useless. Everyone else had run out of the room except for Dr. Jensen. Upshaw was a gigantic man and realized he could take the smaller guy next to him, so he released the gun and quickly rolled to his right, grabbing Dr. Jensen as he fell off the bed and landed on top of the doctor, who was face up.

Upshaw grabbed the doctor's lab coat with his left hand and reared back with his right to smash him in the face with it as the agents started to come into the room. Upshaw looked down at the doctor and was surprised to see not terror but a smile. Unbeknownst to Upshaw, Jensen had practiced this situation hundreds of times. In one motion, he grabbed Upshaw's wrist with his opposite hand, his elbow with the other hand, trapped Upshaw's left leg with his right foot, and thrust his pelvis hard and to the right, winding up on top of the big man.

Haggard saw it all and thought, *Whoa, this guy's good.* Haggard and his team then pounced on Upshaw, maybe a little too hard—but too bad. He'd earned it.

"You guys got this?" asked Dr. Jensen, still on top of Upshaw.

"Yes, sir," was the reply.

"Are you sure? 'Cause I don't wanna have to do this again."

Cocky little shit, thought Haggard as he grinned and shook his head.

NINETEEN

THE FORENSICS TEAM FINISHED their work at Ian Ndobo's house, and now they were back at the Field Office grinding through the details of their search. Agent Alvarez was with the computer techs since that was likely to yield the most useful information.

Ndobo had been very careful to maintain relative anonymity outside of his business. But he wasn't perfect. After a couple of hours, the techs found the contents of a deleted email that hadn't been extra-scrubbed. It was a typical slip. It was too easy to get distracted while deleting emails, but before doing the extra scrub to destroy them completely.

They found an email from England that appeared to contain encrypted information. It was a series of numbers in various lengths, with no obvious pattern. One team began to decipher the message, while another traced the email's origin.

Alvarez asked aloud, "What if this is a book cipher?"

One of the techs looked at him quizzically.

"There was a single book next to the computer. *Native Plants of Florida* or something like that. I thought it was weird, but let's try it." The technician called the room that was processing the other large objects and had the book brought over.

A book cipher is one of the simplest but most secure encryption methods. It works when both parties have the same book. One can then send a message by referencing the page number and the number of the word on a page. Sometimes the addition of a paragraph number is used to facilitate the decryption of the message in the interest of time. The main weakness is that both parties need to have the same edition and printing of the book because there are often format changes or text changes from one edition to the next that would render the cipher useless.

Alvarez knew this and looked at the copyright page. He then called his division's administrative assistant, Sheila Grey. "I need the phone number for Elsevier Books in New York, preferably someone pretty high up in the sales division."

Not only was Grey very good at her job, but she also had a thing for Alvarez. After five minutes, she walked back to Alvarez, holding her personal cell phone. "I have the vice president for sales live on the line, sir."

He raised his eyebrows and nodded his head in a sign of genuine respect.

"Mr. Sellers?" Grey said. "Thank you for holding. I have Special Agent Alvarez here." She handed him the phone. She returned to her office with a little extra sway in her hips, which she hoped he noticed.

He did and also realized he would get to go back to her office to return her phone. Bonus.

"Hello, Mr. Sellers. I have an unusual request I was hoping you could help with."

"I'll try my best. What do you need?"

"I have a book with the title, author, edition, and printing number, and I was wondering if you could give me the sales data on this. Specifically, I want to know if you shipped any to Europe or England, in particular."

Sellers was relieved he wasn't the target of an FBI investigation, near as he could tell. "What are the details of the book now?"

Alvarez gave him the information on the book he had.

"Interesting," Sellers replied. "I bet we didn't ship many of those to Europe. Give me an hour or two to see what we can come up with."

"Thank you, sir. Do you have my number?"

"I do indeed."

"Great. Look forward to hearing back from you." *Hopefully, later this evening*, he thought.

———

As Sam and Tom Jensen drove toward the relatively isolated Venezuelan coast west of Caracas, they came upon a fit-looking man walking toward them. The two Americans were trying to link up with the SEAL team coming from the USS *Georgia* and assumed that whoever was meeting them would fly them out by helicopter.

They slowed the car, and the two parties stared at one another before the man raised his hand in a "stop" motion.

Tom Jensen rolled down his window, and the man asked, "Did you read the article about the commotion in Caracas?"

"Yes, we did," replied Sam. "We have some more information on that with us."

"Then let me in. I'll take you where we leave from."

Two minutes later, they rounded a corner and saw three more men with bags of gear behind a large clump of vegetation overlooking the rocky beach.

"I don't see a helicopter," said Tom.

"Or even a boat," said Sam. "Maybe they have to call for it."

Their new passenger got out and walked over to the three men. After a few seconds of talking, they all looked at the car and continued talking for about a minute. Then their new passenger came over and motioned for Sam and Tom to get out.

"My name is Ace. I heard your comment about the boat," said the new passenger. "We don't have to call for it. We have to go to it."

Sam and Tom scanned the ocean and saw nothing clear to the horizon. They then looked over at the other men who were fishing supplies out of their bags.

Out of one of their bags, they retrieved a folded black rubber thing and a small box with a hose attached to it. Another bag yielded a small black plastic-covered box, followed by a two-foot shaft with a propeller attached to one end. The operator quickly screwed the shaft to the box while his teammate hooked the hose to the rubber object and flipped a switch. The third readied weapons while scanning the surrounding land area for approaching threats.

"Here's the deal," said Ace. "We will be going out to a submarine that is several miles away." Sam raised his eyebrows while Tom started dancing on the beach in anticipation of another adventure.

The now-obvious boat was inflating but looked very small—too small to fit seven men.

"Don't worry. We won't be taking that thing more than a mile, where we have a minisub waiting. We will need to transfer to that, which will take us to the mothership."

"How will we all fit?" asked Sam, looking at the boat.

"We won't. Those guys will stay here and get extracted later. There's room for four men on our boat, although Carlos here will be a little uncomfortable bouncing along curled up on his side. Nice job securing him, though, in that reverse fetal position. I think we'll leave him like that to reduce his temptation to jump overboard. We don't want to waste time having to retrieve someone out of the water."

"When can we leave?" asked Tom, who was now bouncing on his toes. Sam glared at Tom, thinking of all the bad things that could happen with this plan, annoyed that Tom didn't see, or maybe didn't care, about any of them. He then looked over at the boat, which was now inflated and being carried by two men to the water, with the third bringing the motor behind them.

"Right now. Let's get Carlos and whatever small gear you may need. See how close you can get the car to the water. We will need to carry him from there to the boat."

"We have weapons and a backpack, each with the rest of our gear," said Sam. "It's not waterproof, though."

"That's okay. Our minisub will surface long enough for us to transfer everything into it. If it falls overboard, we would leave it anyway."

Sam thought it through quickly and realized it was the best plan on short notice. He jumped into the car and drove it twenty feet from the water's edge before the rocks started shifting under the tires. He stopped and left the keys in it for the three remaining men to use later.

Tom and their SEAL trotted over to the car and opened the trunk to get their backpacks. They pulled Khobulin out of the back seat and laid him on the rocks on his side.

"It looks like the best way to carry him is going to be face down," said Ace.

The Jensens put on their backpacks. Then Sam and Ace each hooked an elbow while Tom grabbed Khobulin's knees. It was awkward, but he found a way to hold them like a wheelbarrow and walk between Khobulin's knees.

A rock gave way under Sam's foot, and he lost his balance and fell, and so did their prisoner face first on the rocks. Khobulin let out a stream of profanities in his native tongue.

"That doesn't sound like Spanish," said Tom.

They picked up the man, who now had blood running from his mouth and nose.

"Sorry, not sorry," said Sam, who felt only a little guilty over enjoying his prisoner in pain.

The other men came to help and loaded the four of them, Khobulin on his side, Sam in the front, with Ace and Tom in the back. They put their packs on top of Khobulin and held their own weapons.

"Ready?" asked Ace as he flipped a switch on the motor. It silently came to life.

Tom looked at him with a question in his eye.

"Electric," said Ace. "If it can power a sedan, it can power a little motor like this, right?"

———

"Mr. Fox from MI-5 on the line for you, sir," said the assistant from the speaker on Frank Burroughs's office phone on the top floor of FBI headquarters in Washington, DC.

He lifted the handset. "Monty, my good friend, that was quick. I hope you have some good news for me."

Montgomery Fox was the head of the British Counterintelligence Service MI-5, and he and Frank Burroughs had coordinated on many cases over the years.

"Right, Frank, I hope so. It seems your Ndobo chap was quite busy during his time here with us."

"Tell me."

"Well, after his conviction for attempting to kidnap a poor lass, he was sent to Her Majesty's Prison Belmarsh, east of London. This is one of our Category A prisons, which has the highest security because we also have many terrorists and other nasty criminals here. Although we have prisoners from the surrounding area as well."

"Go on."

"Our investigation thus far shows Mr. Ndobo naturally assimilated with the other Nigerian prisoners. As you know, these men have very little regard for human life or dignity, and they spend a great deal of their time trying to take advantage of other people in various ways."

Frank was frequently charmed by the British ways of getting to a subject, but sometimes he just wanted the meat, like now.

"And?"

"Well, Mr. Ndobo was a second-generation Nigerian whose parents are still together, and by all accounts, he seemed to have a decent life here. He just let his hormones get away from him one night under the influence of Bombay Bramble Gin. Dreadful stuff, by the way. You'd be best to steer clear of it."

"I'll remember that," replied Frank, who had never heard of it in the first place.

"Anyway, whilst in prison, the other Nigerians filled his head with all kinds of twaddle about how the Europeans and Americans and all capitalists really are actively destroying the Nigerian people and their country."

"Okay." *Get on with it, Monty.*

"They knew he would get out still a young man full of vim and vigor, and so they arranged for him to meet and be mentored by one of their crafty old lions, who would be able to turn his vigor toward their enemy. He ultimately arranged for young Ian to become a travel agent in Florida, and you know his subsequent history better than me now, I'm sure."

"Does this lion have a name, Monty? We *are* trying to track down the origin of all this, you know."

"Quite right, Frank, I almost forgot. His name is Muhammed Agbeni. He attends one of the more radical mosques here in London, where we have tracked a few terror plots originating from."

"Where is he now?"

"That's just it, I'm afraid. We don't rightly know. He was last seen in his council estate, what you Yanks call 'projects,' I'm told, on April 15, the day of the attacks."

"Are you trying to find him?" *Christ, this was like pulling teeth.*

"Oh, most certainly. We have scores of people out 'beating the bushes,' as it were."

"Wonderful. Thank you, Monty. Please let me know as soon as you find out anything."

"Of course, my good man."

Frank decided the charm was best endured over a glass of scotch . . . or three.

———

Joe Park was sweating his suspect hard. The man was initially resistant, but once Park applied the family threat, the suspect lost his willpower fairly quickly. Park knew the North Koreans were naturally paranoid because their tyrannical government made them that way. So it was easy to play on their fears that every government was essentially all-seeing, all-hearing, and all-knowing.

Quickly, he obtained the handler's information and promptly passed it along to his chain of command, who then sent it straight to the CIA. Park didn't know, but the CIA did have several agents in North Korea who were extremely resourceful.

Ji-hoon Kim was ostensibly a mid-level operative in the Reconnaissance General Bureau, also known as Unit 586 of the Korean People's Army. He had induced his still-green subordinate to infiltrate the United States in a container ship that entered the Port of Seattle two months earlier. He used the classic carrot of higher pay if he accepted, mixed with the stick of family shame—and worse if he declined the assignment.

That information was sent to the CIA agents in the field to ascertain its veracity and trace it up the ratline, if necessary, to find its source.

The agents, operating under nonofficial cover, knew that RGB personnel were often actually Chinese operatives injected into the North Korean intelligence service to gather intelligence and actively commit attacks against their opponents, both kinetic and otherwise. So the CIA agents set about trying to find Mr. Kim.

The order first went to Chul Kwan, a native South Korean who came to the United States with his parents twenty-five years ago at the age of ten. At that age, he knew enough about his old country to miss the familiar good parts but was also able to appreciate the significant advantages he had in the United States. More importantly, he could speak both languages like a native. His understandable patriotism for two separate countries was recognized when he attended college at Eastern Washington University. He planned to major in Criminal Justice but took a couple of classes in the Military Science department because they interested him. The chair of that department was Commander Mal-Chin Jang, himself a Korean immigrant who rose through the ranks of the US Navy after graduating with ROTC help ten years earlier. He recognized his own attributes in young Kwan and gradually reeled him into government service. Now Kwan couldn't imagine being anywhere else than the CIA, helping protect both of his countries.

About a year after arriving in the Hermit Kingdom by way of the Yanbian Korean Autonomous Prefecture in northeastern China, Agent Kwan—undercover—had managed to get a job at the Port of Chongjin as a low-level manager for the logistics of freight loading and unloading. Not so coincidentally, the governments of Russia and China both had consulates in Chongjin, a rarity for a North Korean city. His working-class job made it unlikely he would run into his targets at the consulates except during the times of his choosing.

Joe Park's suspect was also from Chongjin, and that is where he'd always been contacted by Ji-Hoon Kim, so Kwan was the natural lead in the investigation. It escaped no one's notice that the proximity to the Chinese border made it an obvious site of Chinese Communist Party activity, both overt and covert.

Kwan was given all the information that the CIA was able to obtain from their files and the internet, which wasn't much, downloaded via secure encrypted burst communications for him to begin his research. He started with the home address that the CIA gave him and began frequenting surrounding businesses in hopes of running across some additional information. In his job at the freight company, he periodically had to make forays to different parts of the city, so it was not suspicious when a bar owner would see a freight worker in his establishment.

Kwan was at a neighborhood bar one evening when a woman with red-rimmed eyes marched in and sat down two chairs over from Kwan. She barked an order at the bartender, who scurried to get her a *nongtaegi*. In South Korea, Kwan knew it as soju, a strong, clear liquor made from corn.

"It's good here," said Kwan, raising his glass of *nongtaegi* as he looked over at her. She was pretty but was getting worry lines around her eyes and mouth.

"I am so tired of this," she said while taking her glass from the bartender and setting it down too hard on the bar, splashing a little of its precious contents out. She looked at it, snorted almost to herself, and then downed about half of it.

"I'm sorry to hear that," said Kwan. "Lots of people are tired of it these days. I have experience with lots of problems as a result. Maybe I can help."

She half-glared at him. "My husband."

"What's he done this time?" He could tell this had been causing her grief for quite some time.

"He leaves at the worst times with no notice. He just gets a call and says he has to go. It doesn't matter what we have going on. Company coming, kid's birthday, it doesn't matter."

"Ouch, that's tough. I'm sorry. How long does he leave for?"

"That's just it. I never know. If he knows, he doesn't tell me. I ask him, and he usually says 'a few hours or a few days,' but sometimes it's a few weeks!"

Kwan winced in sympathy, hoping she'd notice. "What kind of work does he do?"

"He works for the government, some personnel department."

Personnel, thought Kwan. *This sounds more like classified, operational type of work*. He continued commiserating with her until he thought she had no more useful information today. He then announced that he had to get back home to his wife. He paid his tab, gathered his jacket, and stood. "I'll be back through here on a job in a couple of days. I'm free to listen more if you want. Maybe I can think of something between now and then."

She slammed back the rest of her drink and signaled to the bartender for another. "Thanks, I'll think about it. That is if I don't find him and kill him first."

He left and went to his car across the street at the end of the block and got into the driver's seat, and just waited. About twenty minutes later, he saw her exit the bar and walk up the sidewalk away from him. He had a different jacket and hat in the car beside him, so he got those and decided to follow her on foot. Two blocks later, she turned left, and as he rounded the corner, he saw her go into a building at the end of the block. As he approached, he realized it was an apartment building and noted the address. It was the one he was given. He still didn't know her name, but he went to the call box to get an idea of the names of the people who lived there in case he met any later. Of the thirty or so names on the box, he saw the Korean symbology for "Kim, JH" sandwiched between "Kim, JB" and "Kim, JM." Kim was just as common a name in North Korea as in South Korea.

He turned, left the building, and took a circuitous route back to his car. He devised a schedule to do overwatch on the building around his day job and hoped she would show up at the bar in a couple of days.

TWENTY

DR. JOHN JENSEN GOT UP, leaving the HRT guys on top of Upshaw on the floor of the trauma bay. "All right, guess what? We still need to evaluate him since he was in a bad car wreck." That's all he knew. He didn't know who the good guys were at all, although he could tell they were well-trained by their economy of motion, not to mention their lack of body fat.

The rest of the trauma team started filing back into the room, assuming their positions.

"Let's do this," said Dr. Jensen. "From how quickly he jumped off the table, I doubt he is seriously injured. So let's have these guys handcuff his wrists in front of him and his ankles, also. We can lift him to the bed, then resecure each limb to the nearest bed rail. Then we can do our stuff, releasing each individual arm or leg as needed—temporarily."

He stepped aside while the augmented team did just that and started their workup of Upshaw. Haggard stepped up and introduced himself to Dr. Jensen, holding out his hand.

"Thanks for the ground assist," said Jensen once he understood the situation.

"Any time, Doc. Sorry, it had to come down to that, though. We thought he was out of it and didn't think to check for weapons before EMS got there."

"I understand, but I bet you'll do it next time."

Haggard winced, chagrined that this hick doctor thought he could bust his balls. But he also knew that he was right.

"I can tell you ain't from 'round here," said Jensen, drawing out his accent as much as possible. "What agency are you with again?"

"NYPD, but I brought along some FBI friends from New York with me."

"What in the world are you doing so far from home?"

"Believe it or not, we think this guy was instrumental in the Harbor Day attack in New York."

Jensen's eyes grew wide. He then told Haggard about his brother and son in South America, to the amazement of Chuck Haggard.

"Yeah. We really are on the same side here. Let me finish working this guy up. If he has no injuries, I'll release him to you. Just don't kill him in whatever room you take him to. It'll make me look bad, and I'll have to come pay you back."

"You got it, Doc." On the one hand, he was offended that this guy thought he could back that up. On the other hand, he was a little nervous that he might be able to.

"By the way, if you ever want to expand your horizons a little bit, if you know what I mean, I could put a good word in for you with these guys," Haggard said, pointing to the HRT team. He meant it. *Plus, it never hurts to ingratiate yourself with the guys you might need to save your life someday.*

Dr. Jensen finished his workup of Upshaw within an hour and approached Chuck Haggard.

"Believe it or not, we can't find any injuries that merit keeping him in the hospital. He'll have some bruises and aches and pains that'll pop up within the next two days, but nothing life-threatening. If he has pain in a certain area that persists after that, feel free to bring him back. Sometimes we can find small fractures or ligament damage later that weren't evident initially. But remember, we'll be able to tell if he has any new injuries."

Message received, thought Haggard, who then issued orders to his team to load up the prisoner and take him to the nearby fusion center. They did not have a dedicated interrogation room, but he had arranged for a storage room to be used for the effort.

Dr. Jensen's phone buzzed. He retrieved it from his pocket, looked down, and his eyes narrowed. He said quietly, "Oh shit."

Still next to him, Haggard recognized the initial look of alarm on Jensen's face, replaced immediately by one of steely resolve. He saw it regularly in the professionals he worked with daily. He looked at Jensen expectantly.

"This is my wife. She says there is a big mob at the entrance to our subdivision, yelling and banging on the gate. There's a couple of neighbors on the inside with guns, but she's worried they won't have a chance once the gate breaks. And there are no cops in sight. I gotta go."

"Let me send some of my guys with you, Doc." He pointed at three of the HRT guys, motioning them to come over. "They are the best in the business when it comes to this kind of stuff."

"Great, thanks," said Jensen, who then addressed the small team. "Let's go get your gear and head out. Do you have any extra, or do we need to stop at my truck to get mine too?"

———

A couple of days later, Chul Kwan was back in the bar where he had previously met the presumed Mrs. Kim, nursing another *nongtaegi*, when "Mrs. Kim" walked through the door. He pretended not to notice her but watched her body language out of his peripheral vision. She was upset again. He was in a different seat at the bar, and she noticed him and again took a seat two stools down from him. He then made eye contact and feigned pleasant surprise, raising his glass in her direction. She harrumphed, got the bartender's attention, and pointed to Kwan's drink. He scurried to get her another one.

"Good to see you again. How's life?" he asked.

She shook her head as her drink appeared before her. She drank half of it again in one fell swoop. Her eyes welled up with tears, but Kwan couldn't tell if they were from sadness or the drink.

"It's our anniversary today, and I still haven't heard from that poor excuse of a husband."

"Ouch, I'm sorry," replied Kwan. "But I'm sure he is doing something extremely important for the Dear Leader if he can't break away long enough to call his pretty wife."

The corner of her mouth twitched almost enough to be called a smile before settling back down to the scowl she came in with. *Good, that worked*, he thought.

He needed to establish that he wasn't a threat to her. "I've only been married five years to my beautiful wife, so we still try to do something special on our anniversary." He thought that ought to do the trick. But he didn't want to sound too boastful.

"But then again, I don't have near as an important job as your husband. I'm sure he is thinking about you, even if he can't call you." *Nice recovery—thoughtful and humble.*

"Right." She grimaced. "I used to think that, but it just happens too often these years. When he does finally show up, he doesn't even acknowledge that he missed anything."

"Have you ever been to his workplace? Maybe his colleagues could tell you where he is."

"No, he has told me never to come there."

"Not even to bring him lunch when he forgets?"

"Not even then," she answered.

"Would you like to know where he is? I could go there and pretend I'm a government employee who needs something only he can help me with. You said he's with personnel, right?"

"Yes, that's actually a good idea. I can even take you to the building that he showed me once is his building. In fact, I can do it now if you have time. It's not far from here."

Kwan could barely conceal his enthusiasm. He looked at his watch to pretend to study his available time. "I've got time if it's close. I have my next appointment in ninety minutes." *Just long enough for some together-time later, if necessary.*

Fifteen minutes later, she greeted Kwan coming out of the building she had taken him to five minutes earlier. He had a grim look on his face and became more worried.

"I'm afraid I've got bad news," said Kwan, knowing she probably already suspected it. "Nobody in that building knows anyone by his name. Are you sure this is the right building?"

"I'm positive. I even had him point it out to me again about a month after the first time. This is it." Tears started welling in her eyes again as she began to realize her fears were coming true.

"I am so sorry. I've heard of this kind of thing happening to other people but never to anyone I actually knew."

She sniffled and looked at her feet, afraid to make eye contact.

"You know what? You don't need to be alone right now, and I've found it helps a lot to talk this out. Is there a coffee place around here we can go sit quietly?" *Just the right amount of empathy and concern without coming on too strong.*

She thought for a long minute, considering her options, and took a deep breath.

"Yes, I have coffee at my place."

"Are you sure? I don't want him to come home and get the wrong impression."

"He won't have any impression because he won't be back. Besides, my children are with my mother for the day. We can . . . talk undisturbed."

"I can do that, but again I have to leave within the hour to make my next appointment." He hoped he sounded genuinely non-predatory, even though he was inwardly pleased with the prospect of potentially getting closer to this woman. He knew that women were constantly wary of guys trying pickup lines on them, and he didn't want to turn her off just as he was getting closer to his mark.

She sighed again, and he thought, *Maybe I misjudged this, and she wants more from me?*

"Come on, let's go," she said almost too quickly as she turned on her heels and strode off without waiting for him.

Let's go, indeed, thought Kwan as he hurried to catch up to her.

Five minutes later, they were at the building he saw her enter the first day, and she led him to her apartment. She opened the door, and they walked in—and saw her husband sitting at the kitchen table.

———

Tom Jensen saw it first. "What is that?" he asked as he pointed to the eastern sky.

The small black speck loomed larger by the second. Then they saw splashes drawing a line between the plane and their small boat. Then they heard the bangs sounding in time with the splashes. They all realized what was happening simultaneously and jumped out of their boat—except for their prisoner, who was still bound in the reverse fetal position. A split second later, they heard the roar of the twin jet engines underwater after the jet rocketed past them.

They surfaced in time to see the SWCS rise from the water. They saw the inflatable craft they had previously occupied start sinking with their prisoner. Ace swam quickly toward the boat and grabbed the prisoner as the rest swam toward the submersible. Tom and Sam got there first and climbed through the opened hatch as Ace brought Khobulin in. Together Sam and Ace moved Khobulin into the SWCS, and Ace rapidly closed the hatch just as they descended below the water's surface.

By this time, the jet had turned around for another run. He came back to the prior location, firing his guns, but they were already below the surface, nervously awaiting the fatal shot. Fortunately, they only heard a tink as they rapidly descended to a safe depth. Before long, the pilot, who had identified himself as Matt, had relaxed enough to appear normal, guiding the submersible through dark waters back to the *Georgia*.

After mating with the mother submarine, which in the dark appeared magical to Tom and Sam, the occupants transferred to the *Georgia* seamlessly. They were immediately ushered to a room in the rear of the sub, where they were examined by the medical team. Once cleared, they were sent to an adjacent room to be debriefed by the senior intelligence officers of the sub. After Sam was debriefed, he assisted in the questioning of the prisoner.

The captain of the *Georgia* had rapidly descended to 600 feet after collecting the SWCS and its passengers. So they were safe from the Venezuelans, at least. As they headed northward, the interrogations began.

Khobulin was smart enough to recognize that the resources and technology used to apprehend him could also be used to protect him better than he could count on back in Uzbekistan, so he sang like a canary. He gave the physical description of his handler, as well as the approximate dates and times and locations, and methods of communication with him. He gave them the name he used, but none of them believed it was his real name. He also described the contents of the communications, which sent a cold chill through the spines of his interrogators.

They were professionals, though, and dutifully sent the information up the chain.

TWENTY-ONE

AGENT KWAN HAD TO THINK FAST in the face of the woman's husband. All three excuses he could come up with were lame and wouldn't be believed by Kim anyway, so he instantly went to option four—the direct approach.

"Thank Dear Leader, you are here!" exclaimed Kwan as the man's eyes narrowed.

"Your poor wife was worried you would miss your anniversary again," Kwan said, "and was so upset I had to talk her off the ledge, as it were. I told her that us Korean men have a very deep sense of honor that would ensure you would be back before the end of the day—and look!"

Kim had indeed forgotten and was glad the newcomer clued him in. He would have to thank him later. Or kill him.

The next few seconds would be critical, Kwan knew, both for the mission and for his life.

He stuck out his hand and introduced himself using his work name at the freight company. He knew everything he said would be vetted and didn't want to give the impression that he was hiding anything. As he explained in detail how he had met Mrs. Kim, he tried to convey a brotherly concern for her well-being. After a few minutes, he noticed a subtle change in Kim's appearance that indicated he was more relaxed.

Good, he thought. *He either believes I'm no threat, or he just decided he needs to kill me.*

"As I explained to your wife, I have another appointment I need to make soon. But my bladder won't last the long walk. Could I please use your toilet before I leave?"

Kim nodded and pointed to the short hallway that only had two doors. He opened the first one and was relieved to see a men's jacket hanging inside the bathroom door. He fished one of his discreet "button" bugs out of his pocket and applied it to the inside of the crease of the back collar of the jacket. He was glad he had listened to his instructors at the Farm, as the CIA training facility was known, who had pounded into the students the necessity for being ready to apply surveillance at any time, in any fashion. It was easy to explain away a few buttons in one's pocket if he was searched, but these buttons would transmit location and voice data that could be picked up by satellite. He could never go back to see either of them unless invited, which he thought unlikely. He would have to rely on the luck of Kim wearing the jacket.

He urinated, flushed, washed his hands, and returned to the Kims' living room, looking at his watch. "Thank you so much for your hospitality, but I really must leave now for my appointment. They are expecting me by four o'clock." *Maybe he won't kill me right away if he is worried someone might raise suspicion if I don't show somewhere.*

Once the button bug was activated, the signal was immediately acquired by the nearest NSA satellite hovering over the country. There were three focused on different parts of North Korea. A chain of activities was set in motion to track the bug's location and to locate and eavesdrop on any nearby phone or video connections. There was also an ability to do voice analysis to try to identify the principals involved.

———

Chuck Haggard's team got a police escort from the hospital to the fusion center at the Texas Department of Public Safety Headquarters so traffic lights wouldn't inconvenience them. Haggard chose the fusion center as the site for the interrogation of Upshaw because of the myriad connections that were instantly available with other governmental agencies. He could use these to verify or immediately investigate anything Upshaw might divulge.

He thought about taking him to a military base that would have better security, but the unfettered access to other agencies was more important. He figured the muscle on his team could provide enough security, and he easily convinced the local commander of the center to establish an outer perimeter as well.

On arrival, the hallways were lined with people like a gauntlet to see the man who may have perpetrated the Harbor Day attacks. Haggard briefly talked with the commander of the fusion center, asking him to send reinforcements to the subdivision where Dr. Jensen made his home.

"I would love to, sir, but I'm putting out literal fires all over the city with people burning and looting grocery and convenience stores. I have nobody to spare."

"Copy that," said Haggard, who then radioed the info to his HRT teammates who were with Dr. Jensen. He hoped the doctor was as good with firearms as he was with his hands, should the need arise.

Upshaw, still in his hospital gown, was taken to the room and sat in a chair, his hands and feet still shackled. Haggard thought it would be best to keep him both distracted, which a hospital gown always does to people, and unable to access another weapon he may have secreted in his clothing they hadn't found yet.

"All right, Jack," Haggard said to the shackled suspect.

Upshaw looked up with his eyebrow raised. "Yes, we know your name, date of birth, occupation, address, affiliation with 415, and your mother's maiden name." It was a not-so-subtle reminder that his family was potentially at risk if he didn't cooperate.

"Start at the top and tell us everything."

"I don't know what you're talking about," came the expected weak reply.

"I thought you would say that. So here goes. Tell me about Andrei Chikatilo."

Upshaw started to sweat.

"I see you know him. So obviously, you know what he can do to you if we let him know you've spent some time with us. Or maybe what he can do to your family."

Upshaw placed his forehead down on his hands, trying to think of a way out of this. He truly hated the US government and wanted to bring them down in any way possible.

"I want a lawyer."

"Fine, have it your way." Haggard turned to a companion. "Mitch? Get Chikatilo on the phone for me while we wait for Upshaw to go through the phone book here to look for a lawyer that won't be able to help him anyway." He happened to have found a five-year-old local phone book in a drawer. It landed with a thud in front of Upshaw's nose. "Good luck finding one here in Austin who's an expert in international terrorism that can help you get out of the crime of the century."

Upshaw thought for another minute, shook his head almost imperceptibly, realized he was out of options, and took a deep breath.

That didn't take long, thought Haggard. *Either I'm getting real good at this, or this guy is a real amateur. Probably both.*

Time for one last negotiation. "Okay, what will you do for me if I tell you everything?"

"We won't execute you for treason against the US." Haggard thought he could back that up. "But you will face prison, no way out of that. How much time will depend on the prosecutor and how much useful information you give us. Of course, if you give us shit, it will be worse for you. Capisce?"

Being from New Jersey, Upshaw understood *capisce.* He took another deep breath and exhaled loudly. "Okay, here's what I know. I got contacted by Chikatilo a year or two ago through my dark web channel."

"Gimme the details." Haggard wanted to make sure he wasn't missing another dark web channel.

"He said he was looking for help with a problem in our area. He said a ship would be coming through that didn't need to dock."

"Didn't need to dock? What does that mean?"

"Well, he asked to meet me face-to-face, so we arranged a meeting about a month after the first contact. He knew I was a harbor pilot in addition to my work in 415. He said he wanted to deprive the government of the tax revenue from this ship, and he thought the best way to do that would be to abandon it in the harbor's main channel. He wanted me to offload the crew into our harbor pilot vessel after I placed the ship in the most critical spot."

"Didn't you think offloading the crew would be a good way to get them off a soon-to-be exploding ship?"

"I didn't know they would blow it up! I thought they would just leave it in the way, causing a massive marine traffic jam. It would take time to investigate what happened, find an appropriate crew to move it out of the way, process the cargo—all of that. The shipping business runs—or it ran—on a very tight schedule. The resulting backup of goods going through the Port of New York/New Jersey would take weeks to unwind, which in turn slows down the tax revenues the government collects. This is the kind of stuff we did as part of 415—encourage uncooperativeness with tax collectors of all kinds. This was really no different."

"Okay, give me all the details of your meeting with Chikatilo, location, date, time, his appearance, clothing, transportation, communication channels, how he paid you, everything."

Haggard wrote down the answers and handed them to his assistant to verify the information he had just been given. He had more questions. "Did he give you any other contact info besides the dark web channel? Any other channels? Phone number? Another alias?"

Upshaw began to realize he had been duped by the feds when Haggard threatened to get Chikatilo on the phone. He had no way of contacting him. He thought he might have a chance of getting out of the bind he was in as long as he could figure out a way to give the feds some helpful information. But he would be sure to make it very long and hard for them to act on that information.

———

In London's East End, Muhammed Agbeni was hiding in the back bedroom of a friend's ground-floor flat when suddenly the front and rear doors were rammed open, and ten heavily armed officers in body armor rushed in. For all the pride the Brits have about not arming their beat cops, they don't hesitate to provide the firepower and training for a few elite teams.

They quickly found Agbeni, secured him, and grabbed his nearby laptop and phone. Then they bundled him into their van and whisked him off to Scotland Yard.

The interrogators did not waste time. They immediately showed Agbeni photos of his entire family, including his grandchildren, being perp-walked into Belmarsh prison.

"Mr. Agbeni, I won't drag this out. You know why we're here. For every piece of truthful information you give us, we'll release a member of your family. Start talking."

———

The National Security Council met for their regular update, and the president asked as he walked in, "What's new today?"

Danielle Haverford, the DHS secretary, spoke first. "Well, sir, we are acquiring information on multiple fronts."

"Finally," said the exasperated president.

"FBI has located a North Korean they think may be involved in Seattle. They are interrogating him now."

The president's eyes narrowed, thinking of the thunderous denunciations he was going to have to endure from the other side after making overtures at friendship with the Hermit Kingdom.

"And they have also found a lead that may be important in Miami. They found a boat motor transom who they traced to a charter deep-sea fishing boat owner down there who can't be found. The last name on his reservation list was a man who also can't be found."

"Interesting," said the president. "Go on."

"The man is a Briton named Ian Ndobo."

"Am I supposed to know who that is?" interrupted the president.

"No, sir, but our colleagues at MI5 do. He was in prison there for five years for the attempted kidnapping of a young girl."

"Okay, so he's a jerk. How does that lead to him being here?"

"Our friends tell us that the prison he was in is a hotbed of revolutionary types that is notorious for having its 'graduates' go on to commit a variety of political crimes. We are still chasing down all leads related to this, but it will take quite some time."

"Great," said the president. "What else?"

"Our team from New York, the hybrid FBI/NYPD team, is in Texas and may have captured one of the people involved in the Port of New York/New Jersey attack, a 415 leader named Jack Upshaw."

The president frowned. He couldn't fathom a connection between all these. "Okay, anything else?"

"Yessir, our team in Venezuela has a person of interest who may be involved in the Houston attack in custody. This one is tricky. They are making their way to a hopefully isolated area of the coast to be picked up by a SEAL team and taken back to their submarine. We hope to have more information on them by tomorrow."

"Okay, I can't see a connection between the people you just talked about. Can anyone else here see one?"

"No, sir, not yet," replied the national security director. "But we are diligently exploring not just these but many other leads. We hope to have some actionable information within twenty-four and forty-eight hours."

TWENTY-TWO

DR. JENSEN DROVE THE GOVERNMENT SUV as the HRT team geared up again. He had to stop at his truck to get his gear, since the team had no extras. He explained the layout and the info he had so far. "There is only one entrance to the gated subdivision, but it is blocked by the mob. There is no way to get in that way without letting them all in. I'm going to drive to a church behind the subdivision that has a parking lot just above a neighbor's unfenced backyard. We can get to his driveway, then the streets from there.

"We have a few of the neighbors who have guns," Dr. Jensen said, "but not a lot of training in how to use them. I'll call up one of them at the gate to tell them we are coming in behind them. I'll have my wife grab a bunch of 5.56 ammo to stage if we need extra. I'll let you guys decide how to handle the big crowd and where you want to position the rest of us. And I'll show you an elevated area that's also protected that might be good for overwatch."

Damn, this is a doctor? thought the senior HRT member. He pointed at his teammate in the left rear seat, who nodded his understanding that he was overwatch today.

A few minutes later, they came to the church parking lot and checked their comms as Dr. Jensen bounced down the backyard and hit the neighbor's driveway roughly, showering sparks on the concrete. He sped through the streets toward the gate area and slowed about a block away at the elevated area. The overwatch team member jumped out expertly with his gear, instantly found the best position, and set up.

The two armed neighbors were about halfway between them and the gate where the mob was yelling, banging on the gate, and pacing back and forth, testing it and looking for vulnerable areas in and around it. They looked a lot like wild animals at the zoo.

Jensen screeched to a halt behind his neighbors, who were relieved when they saw three heavily armed, kitted-out men jump out of the vehicle. They were surprised to see Dr. Jensen as one of them in body armor, also carrying an AR-15.

"John, is that you?" asked the smaller man, holding his AR-15 without a sling. It looked brand new, as opposed to Jensen's scratched-up model. He wondered if the man had ever shot it, much less trained with it.

"Hey Steve, what's going on here?"

"Well, this mob made their way here about half an hour ago and has been growing in size ever since. They're saying they are hungry and want whatever we have. They started out asking somewhat politely, but as time passes and their size increases, they are getting more belligerent."

"What are you doing for defense so far?"

"Bill and I are it for now." Jensen had already noticed the other neighbor carrying a nice bolt-action hunting rifle. "Everyone else is still at work. The spouses and kids who are home are all behind locked doors."

"How are you for ammo?" Jensen estimated the mob now numbered about two hundred people.

"I've got what's in my magazine, about thirty rounds. Bill has a box of 30.06 in his pocket. We are sure glad to see you guys. Who are those guys, anyway? I don't recognize that SUV you're driving. Is that new?"

"These are some new friends I made at work. They're with the FBI, Hostage Rescue Team."

Bill's mouth was opened for several seconds as he considered the possibilities. "Are any families here being held hostage?"

"These guys are trained in the use of nonlethal as well as lethal means to solve problems like this. Essentially the whole neighborhood is being held hostage since this is the only entrance that this mob thinks is available. And to answer your question, the vehicle is theirs. I just drove it because I knew the rough access from the church down to Don's driveway, and they needed to kit up anyway."

The crowd started pushing and shaking against the gate, their yelling getting louder. The gate was fairly stout but, at this rate, would be breached within thirty minutes.

"Okay," said Jensen. "We need to dissuade them from attacking the gate. Once it goes, we'll be overwhelmed in seconds. Plus, I bet there are already bangers in that crowd starting to explore the perimeter. That's what I would do."

Bill hadn't thought about that yet, and his face paled.

"Stay here. I'm going to talk to the HRT crew and then come back to talk to the mob through the gate. Don't shoot me in the back."

Jensen explained the situation to the nearest HRT member, who nodded understanding and positioned himself and his other forward teammate to the maximum tactical advantage with fairly clear, but protected, lines of fire toward the mob. He also notified his overwatch partner of the plan, who was already looking at members of the mob periphery looking at other areas of the fence.

Jensen then realized that if the rest of the neighborhood were as poorly armed as the two guys in front of him, they were sitting ducks. He called his wife, who was staging the ammo at another neighbor's house a block away. "Hi, Babe, we've got two hundred people at the front gate trying to break in, and Bill and Steve are the only other armed guys in the neighborhood. They're both here, which means all other access points are unsupervised. I, fortunately, brought three heavily armed, trained guys with me from work, but we are going to be busy with this crowd. I need you to call everyone in the neighborhood to converge on your location in that house. It will be easier to defend that way. And have them pass the word to other neighbors to do the same and bring whatever weapons, ammo, food, and water they can grab quickly. You might be there awhile."

"On it," she replied and instantly went to her neighborhood group text to relay the information far more efficiently than her husband ever could have by calling people.

Jensen then walked down to the gate with his two neighbors behind him and on either side by about fifty feet. He stood about twenty feet from the gate with his rifle at low-ready.

"This is private property!" he shouted.

"Come on, man. We just want some food. I got babies at home," yelled one of the mobsters. "We know y'all got a lot of food!" screamed another.

"We don't have anything for you. But the Walmart on 360 just got a shipment in. You can go there. I heard they're not even making people pay for it."

About a third of the group started peeling off in that direction. *Good*, thought Jensen. *Every little bit helps. It will take them a while to figure out I was making this up.*

Of those that remained, about half were unsure if they wanted to go or not. They were hedging their bets by looking for direction from the others at the gate.

Jensen thought it best to use the direct approach next. "Any attempt to come through that gate will be met with force. We've got heavily armed guys watching everything and everybody, just waiting for an excuse . . ."

Fortunately, the carrot and stick approach began to work. The yelling and rocking of the gate became less threatening as the mob looked everywhere from their side of the gate, trying to find the other soldiers.

"Your friends that left are going to get all the food at the Walmart. You better hurry up and get there to get your share."

The teammate on overwatch had been in communication with the fusion center, giving them a running description of the situation. They had found a couple of patrol cars that were otherwise free and sent them to the neighborhood.

The siren from the closest patrol car was faint at first but gradually intensified. Then another one from the other direction also got louder. This seemed to convince the wavering half of the remaining crowd to move on. Once the ones that were left realized they were substantially weakened, they began to move off as well.

———

Once the button bug on Kim's jacket was activated in North Korea, a signal was immediately transmitted into the air in an encrypted burst mode, giving its location and the status of its battery and voice recording capability. From there, it would stay inactive unless moved or it picked up voices. Then it would repeat the process every five minutes or so. It had a battery life expectancy of about a year under normal circumstances, so if it quit transmitting, it was because it was in an out-of-the-way place or someone found and disposed of it. It could be pinged to rule out the first possibility.

The signal was routed by satellite to the SigInt section of the NSA in Washington, DC. Another technician on Nancy Anderson's team announced, "We have a new listening device just activated in the northern part of North Korea, in the city of Chongjin. Systems are all green."

Anderson responded, "Copy that. Let's get a Korean specialist in here to assist. We'll need three in total, so once they are here, we'll brief them and then let them set up their shift rotation. Also, make sure all the output from the device is recorded so we can review it and call in additional translators as necessary." Her assistant next to her picked up the nearest phone to make the calls.

The button bug also had a "sniffer" function that could pick up signals from surrounding cell phones and relay those as well. Fifteen minutes later, the bug transmitted a phone number. "We've got a new number associated with the North Korean bug," the assistant said, and he logged it in. This now enabled the NSA to get any number that this phone called or received. They did not know who this belonged to or why they were getting this information, only that it was important enough to the US government to risk someone's life to place it, so they needed to treat it as if thousands, maybe millions, of lives depended on it.

"Foreign language spoken—male, label A," announced the tech. He checked his monitors. "Looks like it's Korean. . . . Recording function is operative." Not only would it record the voice, but the technology also created an electronic voiceprint based on the shape of the sound wave. This way, any future conversation that involved this person could automatically be assigned to him in real time based on his voiceprint. In addition, it was able to access the phone microphone at all times, not just when he made or answered a call. Now they had to wait for the Korean specialists to arrive in their DC office.

Twelve hours later, Kwan was able to get out an encrypted burst message that identified the target and his apartment location. By then, Anderson's team had identified the owner of that phone number as "Ji-Hoon Kim." When Kwan's transmission was decrypted and shared with the team in DC, it confirmed that their information so far was accurate. The CIA also shared that this was a major suspect in the Harbor Day attacks and thus may be related to their focus on Venezuela.

That information amped up Anderson and her team's focus. The Korean specialists were in a groove now, relaying basic info every thirty minutes, with the understanding that if something they deemed important came up, they would inform her immediately. So far, the only conversations had been those of daily life, including the few phone calls he made or received.

"We have a new number called," announced the technician monitoring Kim's phone. "This one's in Beijing. Working on provenance and exact location now."

The Korean specialist on duty spoke up, "My Chinese is okay, but it would be helpful to have a native speaker in here also."

"I agree," said Anderson, nodding to her assistant, who instantly picked up the phone.

It was now 0400 in Chongjin, so any phone calls made at that hour had to be unusually important. Indeed, Kim spoke Chinese to the recipient.

The Korean specialist offered up his interpretation of the conversation. "It seems he is asking for information on a person. I didn't catch the name."

"It doesn't matter," said Anderson. "No one calls Beijing at 0400 to chitchat. This guy is dirty. Get this to CIA, now." She motioned to the CIA liaison, who reached for her phone as the Chinese specialist walked in.

———

Muhammed Agbeni was in an interrogation room in Scotland Yard—his hands cuffed to an iron half-circle welded to the table in front of him.

Only one man was sitting across from him, but there was another, bigger man a few feet to his right. To his left was a full-length mirror embedded within the wall, no doubt hiding live observers behind the one-way glass.

"Mr. Agbeni," the interrogator said, "please save us both loads of time getting the information we need. Your lovely family would greatly appreciate it also." The interrogator had spread out fifteen pictures of various members of his family on the table in front of him, along with the book *Native Plants of Florida* that they had taken from his home. He then knew they had proof of his involvement in the Harbor Day attacks.

"And remember, each piece of information you give us will need to be verified before we let each family member out. Of course, that will take time, so the quicker you go, the shorter their stay will be as our guests. And because we are not animals, we will let you decide who will be the first to be released."

The unspoken but mutually understood implication was that the last few family members released would suffer the most. And knowing his favorite was the first released will make them realize they were the opposite, thus sowing seeds of discontent within his organization.

Agbeni had been an inmate in Belmarsh before. To say it was an awful experience would be putting it lightly. The constant cacophony; the fights all around him; the regular threats to his life; the cold, tasteless food; the even colder steel beds; and the open steel toilets turned strong men into savages and destroyed weak ones. But he had endured the suffering because he was a warrior. The rest of his family understood what he did, but they were not warriors. He couldn't imagine his wife, or his granddaughters, having to suffer such indignities at the hands of infidels.

"Where would you like me to start?"

———

"Mr. President, we believe we are now getting some helpful information regarding the origination of the Harbor Day attacks," said Neil Iglesias, the director of national intelligence, to open the latest meeting of the National Security Council. It was his job to coordinate and coalesce the multiple streams of intelligence from different collecting agencies worldwide to, it was hoped, prevent another 9/11. The prevention aspect was long gone with the Harbor Day attacks, but the position was still useful in finding the perpetrators through every means possible.

The president nodded in his direction.

"FBI has found a connection between what they think is the PortMiami suicide boater and a known Nigerian radical Muslim instigator in Britain. They found traces of an email thread between them on suicide guy's computer and evidence of a probable book cipher using a book at his residence and an identical one shipped by special request to a bookstore near this guy's residence in London. He disappeared on the day of the attacks, but MI-5 just found him. He's apparently talking to them, but it will be a while before they can verify his info."

"I was hoping you would have something concrete by now, Neil."

"I understand. If you bear with me, I think you will find this helpful."

The president sighed deeply and leaned back in his chair, already becoming bored with this circuitous storytelling. But he knew he had to let them justify their conclusions to the other members at the meeting, if for no other reason than to create a paper trail for everyone's protection.

"CIA traced a contact of the Port of Seattle attack to a North Korean intelligence operative, whose base is very close to the Chinese border. They have started a surveillance op on him. Most likely, it will lead to a Chinese handler, but we need some more time to confirm."

"Go on."

"Our fusion center in Austin, Texas, under the field control of a hybrid NYPD-FBI team, has custody of the guy we believe is responsible for the Port of New York and New Jersey attack, a guy named Jack Upshaw, who is a leader in the 415 movement."

"Again, I don't see anything connecting any of these," exclaimed the president, getting more exasperated by the minute.

"We've been looking at all of these guys, trying to find a common denominator, and we think we have found it. We have descriptions and some limited encrypted contact information about this handler. Through our facial recognition algorithms and forensic electronic communications abilities, we have found that all of these guys have had contact in the last year with an Eastern European man."

"Who is he? And where is he?"

"Defense got information from the Venezuelan team of SEALs, the FBI agent, and his nephew who were extracted from there recently. It turns out they were able to capture a guy that may be the handler of the Port of Houston attack perpetrators. His name is Nikolai Khobulin, and he is a known Uzbeki agent who formerly worked for the KGB. He says that his handler was meeting with him in Caracas when he realized he was about to get disappeared. Then all hell broke loose. It turns out that this handler matches the description of the man all these other people had contact with."

"Awesome, let's send a missile into his last known location and be done with this," said the president.

"That would be nice, except for the fact that he had told Khobulin that there were pre-positioned containers on the streets of a few major US cities that held weapons of mass destruction. An electronic kind of dead-man's-switch controls them. If he doesn't send the appropriate codes to these on a regular basis, they will release their destructive material."

"Which is?" The president was getting irritated now with so little information.

"We don't know exactly. Nor do we know the type of container or the cities that were unwittingly hosting them."

"Why not, dammit?" The president pounded the table with his open palm. "This is ridiculous!"

"Sir, the man did not give Khobulin the details. He thinks it was information shared with him in a comradely way, implying that Khobulin would be paid handsomely to defuse these if the handler achieved his objective. He said it in a way to gain his buy-in with the project. Almost like he was a fellow combatant against a common enemy. Furthermore, we don't know if this man is under the control of a higher-level actor."

Iglesias went on, "For these reasons, Mr. President, we need to find this man and capture him alive."

TWENTY-THREE

"ALL RIGHT, GENTLEMEN," said Captain Scott Cooper of the USS *Georgia* to the assembled SEALs and officers of the boat in the Officers' mess, as well as Sam and Tom. It was the only secure space big enough to have such a conversation on the boat, which was now 700 feet below the ocean's surface near Aruba. It was definitely safe from Venezuelan ears, but they always worried about a possible spy in the ranks, thus necessitating the secure meeting room.

"The brass thinks a high-ranking manager of the Harbor Day attacks may have recently been in Caracas, where he was interrogating our new prisoner when everything went sideways." Cooper started passing out to the group sketches of the man in question.

"We have been tasked with finding this man, capturing him alive, and remanding him back to the US for further questioning." He looked at the group, man by man. "We have been authorized to launch another drone now for intelligence purposes pre-mission." The captain pointed at the officer in charge of the drone program on the sub, who then scurried off to find his second-in-command to get the ball rolling. "I'm going to leave the operational details to the guys doing the hard work here. Once you get a plan, let me know the specifics, okay?"

———

Colonel Alberto Flores finished his meeting in Caracas, which turned out to be perfunctory. The higher-ups congratulated him for identifying the intruding aircraft and then dispersed to organize their response. They left him to his own devices with no further instructions other than to get back to Maracaibo, which made him even more nervous.

He quickly called his wife to activate their escape plan by code word and then drove in one of the base's vehicles to think about his options. He correctly assumed that if he went straight back to Maracaibo, he would be permanently incapacitated, one way or another. He headed west out of Caracas along the coast.

After an hour of randomly driving into and out of towns along the coast road, he came to a relatively deserted area of low-lying dunes. He caught a flicker of movement out of his right eye. As he turned his head to see what it was, he counted eight scuba divers coming out of the water with bags.

He slowed as he contemplated the meaning of what he was seeing. Dive tourists wouldn't have all those bags, and locals wouldn't have that many people to help harvest the shellfish. That left only one answer.

That the Americans would be there wasn't much of a surprise. As he thought about it more, he realized that all the exits out of the country would be manned by personnel specifically looking for him. So he needed to get out surreptitiously. He quickly decided that the most undetectable exit would be by the submarine these divers had come from.

He parked his car behind a native grass-covered dune and got out. Realizing he still had his military uniform on and that it might elicit a silenced gunshot as a form of greeting, he took off his shirt and his underlying white tank top, which he used to wave with one upheld hand as he came out from behind the dune.

———

"Contact, twelve o'clock," said Ace to the rest of the crew. He dropped to one knee and swung his silenced carbine to point at the man walking toward them with both arms up, one holding a white piece of cloth. Five team members instantly took up similar positions facing outward to provide a 360-degree defensive position. The other two were Tom and Sam Jensen, who fumbled around to join the rest but didn't know where to aim.

The SEALs on board the *Georgia* had decided the best way to capture their subject was with a team of eight, which required two SWCS units. Once they realized that Tom's Spanish language skills were better than theirs and that he and Sam had seen the compound and at least some of the conspirators, they agreed to take the pair with them. Fortunately, Tom and Sam were Scuba certified.

However, they were frozen with this interloper interrupting their plans.

"Tom, ask him what he's doing here. He is military and knows we are too."

Tom started the conversation in Spanish, translating for the Americans as he went.

"My name is Colonel Alberto Flores. I am with the Venezuelan Air Force. You are the Americans with the drone, no?" He was on thin ice here, and he knew it. He continued talking. "I saw it when I was flying yesterday and sent the fighter to shoot it down. But my superiors don't trust me. They will have me killed. I am leaving Venezuela. I am not coming back. I have sent my family away. But I can help you against my government first."

Ace, the squad leader, made a decision. "Do you have a vehicle?" They didn't have time to kill him and hide the body, so they would have to take him with them.

"Yes, it is behind the grass over there. But it is not big enough for you all."

"No problem. I'll send three of my men with you to find another vehicle." He pointed at Tom and two of his SEALs. "Go find one big enough for four men, and then come back here." He decided to let Flores think they were there to overthrow the rulers.

Thirty minutes later, they returned with another car. They loaded their gear in the trunk but kept their weapons and got into the vehicles, with one of the SEALs driving Flores's car, along with Ace and Tom.

They headed back into Caracas toward the compound Tom and Sam had just left, not knowing if their target—Khobulin's handler—was still there.

One hour later, they approached the compound in the vehicles and split to drive around it, meeting on the other side.

"Flores, do you know this place?" asked Ace.

"Yes, this is off-limits to us. I've heard they pay a lot of money to the brass to keep everyone out."

"We need to get in there and find one man." He outlined the plan.

Two minutes later, the two cars were on opposite sides of the compound, and the nearby video cameras were shot out. They parked the cars next to the walls, and the men used them to climb up and over the compound walls. Once over the walls, they moved silently to converge on the main building that Khobulin had escaped from. Flores went with them, knowing he would be a dead man without their protection. Plus, his military uniform might give them an advantage.

They reached the building and surrounded it, peering in the windows to get as much info as possible while trying to stay within cover whenever possible. They were surprised there was no outside security.

There was no activity inside, as near as they could tell. Ace sent the other team to the back door while his team took the front. They checked the doors and found them unlocked. They entered simultaneously and efficiently went through the building. There was no one in the main room, and they cleared the two small rooms quickly. It looked like the occupants had left quickly, leaving things strewn about. Tom saw a phone on the floor in one corner, retrieved it, and gave it to Ace.

"Do you think this might help?"

"It might." He keyed his mike to communicate via the overhead drone with his contact on a fishing trawler fifteen miles off the coast. "I've got no joy at the compound, but we found a phone that may be the one that was tracked by NSA. It's password protected, and we're going through every six-digit combination sequentially, but it will take us a while to get it. Can you see if they can identify it? If so, it may lead to the handler once we get into his contacts."

"Roger that," came the response from the trawler. "Standby."

The DOD liaison relayed the information to Nancy Anderson's team at the NSA, who confirmed the location was that of the tracked phone.

They used their superior computational power to go through the password combinations much faster than the team on the ground.

It was a well-kept secret that drone technology had advanced to the point that they could now receive and send signals of all wavelengths stealthily.

———

As one of the team members on the ground was punching in numbers on the phone, it suddenly opened up to its Home Screen. "Boss, we're in."

"Great," said Ace. "Find the contacts, and let's see if we get lucky."

Once in, he showed the contacts to Flores. "Do any of these look out of the ordinary to you? Like maybe not local?"

Flores scrolled through, looking at both names and numbers. Finally, he came to a one-name contact with a foreign number. "This one is not normal."

"Okay, if we call it from this number, he won't pick up because he will know it is compromised. Make sure your outgoing caller ID is blocked. Then use your phone to call this number. He might pick up, and we can start tracking it." Ace relayed the plan and the suspected phone number to his contact, who passed it along.

———

"We've got a new number to track," announced Anderson to her team in Washington. "Let's find out where he is."

The technicians went to work quickly on the satellites, tracking audio, visual, and electronic information.

TWENTY-FOUR

DEMYAN WAS HEADING TOWARD the harbor to get on a boat he had hastily arranged to get him out of Venezuela. Even though he'd paid a lot of protection money to the Venezuelan government over the years, he was worried the Americans could outbid him at the airport, and his protectors would instantly change their loyalty.

He neared the harbor and was searching for the boat from the road when his phone rang. He picked it up, thinking it was his boss.

"Ja," he spoke into it as he looked for the boat. Silence. He looked at the phone to see the number. No ID. "Hello?" *Must be a bad connection.*

"We've got him," announced the SigInt technician in Washington. "He's at the harbor." The technicians relayed the location information to the team on the ground in Venezuela, who quickly consulted their digital maps. Anderson's team was also able to share the real-time location of the phone on their maps.

Ace said to the team, "Here's the plan. My car will approach from the west." He pointed to the driver of the other car. "You take your car to the east of the harbor but drop off three guys near the middle. The first team to identify him, develop a plan to capture him." Then, pausing to open the door to other ideas, something he firmly believed led the special ops program to greater effectiveness, he asked, "Does anyone have a better idea?"

The team members shook their heads.

"All right, let's do it." The two teams split, hustled back over the walls to their cars, and made their respective ways to the harbor.

———

Demyan now realized that his phone was an anchor, not a lifeline, and would lead to his demise. He pulled into the parking lot facing the beach in La Guaira. To his left was a sports complex with a baseball field with covered bleachers and the marina containing his boat contact beyond it. There was a lot of activity in front of the baseball diamond, with about a hundred people gathered around a drum line, dancing to the beat and cheering. They appeared to be cheering on an arriving little league team. Demyan approached them from behind and began mimicking their dancing while searching the crowd. A minute later, he saw what he needed and headed toward a young couple with a stroller. While doing so, he removed the phone and cleared the small contact list and the call and message history.

The father was leaving the field entrance carrying a toddler while looking away from the stroller and cheering on his son. They must have won. Demyan took that opportunity to stealthily place his phone behind the rear cushion of the man's stroller.

Demyan then headed toward the marina at a pace not quite fast enough to look out of place. He patted his jacket pocket. Reassuringly, it was still there.

He always carried an extra burner phone programmed with only the most essential numbers. He had bought and programmed it one day in Cucuta when he left his main phone at his house in San Cristobal. He was careful to keep it charged but never turned it on again to prevent it from being tracked.

He came to the location previously given to him and announced, "Señor Fuerte?" A bald head emerged from the cabin.

"Si, señor, where would you like to go today?"

Demyan glanced beyond the man back down the sidewalk he'd come from and felt reassured that there wasn't anything out of the ordinary. "I'll tell you when we get out of the harbor. Are you ready to go?"

"I am."

"Very good. I'll cast off the lines while you start her up. Turn off your transponder first." Thirty seconds later, they were underway.

It was about an hour's drive to the marina from their location in Caracas, and as the two teams made their way impatiently through the typical big-city traffic, they followed the tracker on their cell phones. The target made its way slowly around the area of the baseball field and visited several businesses in the area, starting with an ice cream shop. The teams identified the precise spots they would start their foot searches, but suddenly the target began moving faster toward the east.

The voice from the fishing trawler came over their earpieces. "Be advised—the target seems to have gotten into a car that is moving east along the coast road. We are trying to identify it now."

"Roger that, we are tracking also," one of the team members responded.

They were leaving Caracas and had a single winding road to travel to La Guaira, where the marina was. They wanted to catch the vehicle while it was still in town so that they had more options. If it left town to the east, they would be more limited in their approach.

Anderson's team at the NSA had been split to include the possible Chinese connection, so the remainder was focused on the reliable cell phone signal in La Guaira. No one had been monitoring the video signal from the satellite feed since that was a lot more labor-intensive. Once the speed of the target signal matched that of a vehicle, they addressed the satellite video feed again, with the responsible technician rotating his chair to face the appropriate monitors.

"Give me fifteen minutes, and I'll have the vehicle description for you," said Anderson to her DOD liaison.

"Chief, we have the provenance of the Beijing phone."

"Go ahead," Anderson answered.

"It belongs to a Mr. Zhao Yi. He was a state councilor until about 2018, when he was removed from office for some reason."

Anderson pointed to the State liaison, who got on his phone, as did the CIA liaison.

"Well, this just got even more interesting," said Anderson to Stan Inaka, who had just arrived early for his shift. Anderson was operating on very little sleep, so she and Inaka arranged to do twelve-hour shifts. Since the Far East was about twelve hours ahead in time zones, and Inaka had Asian roots that might help him identify important patterns quicker than Anderson, he offered to work during the time that those in the Far East would be more active during the day—which meant he worked nights. Even though night shift work was hard in any industry, and it was harder the more years under one's belt, he relished being back in the thick of the action.

Anderson explained the developments as Inaka donned his headset and started his shift. One by one, the oncoming technicians took over from their colleagues, who quickly briefed them individually, anxious to go home after their long shift. As any shift worker in the world knows—despite the best protocols and intentions of those involved, things still get overlooked during the shift change report on a regular basis.

TWENTY-FIVE

ZHAO YI PONDERED THE MESSAGE he had received on his emergency phone in Beijing. It included a single code word that meant "problem." Ji-Hoon Kim didn't believe in coincidences; nor did Zhao, who had publicly been removed as state councilor in 2018. He had been secretary general of the State Council, similar to the president's Cabinet in the United States, and the move had been orchestrated to make foreign governments think he had been taken out of play. In reality, he became the shadowy director of special projects the Chinese president ordered to be carried out discreetly, generally to subvert foreign governments.

Zhao had previously recruited Kim in the DPRK to work outside the typical chain of command to establish agents in the United States to cause problems for US authorities. These approaches were quite variable and creative. Some involved teams that explored disrupting the electrical grid. Randomly shooting large transformers at generating plants or substations was a favorite tactic. Breaking into water systems via poor electronic security was another. Interfering with train routing, either physically or electronically, was becoming popular as well. Over time, the goal was to create doubt in the minds of ordinary Americans that their government could manage the day-to-day infrastructure. It was not a stretch to associate incompetence with illegitimacy, and a major cause of instability within a country arose from the frustration of the population with its leaders.

In addition, Zhao believed that sowing seeds of discontent in the United States would further China's goal of becoming the predominant world power, since leaders dealing with multiple domestic problems had less time, energy, and money to focus on other threats.

Zhao recalled his meeting with the European, who gave his name as "Bludnik," about a year ago, where he was pitched a unique proposition.

"We have a mutual desire to make things difficult for the US," Bludnik had said. "My employer has a silent major ownership stake in the Port of Los Angeles. We would like for that to be more profitable. Our major competition is the Port of Seattle. We would like for them to be inoperative for a long time. When they become insolvent, we will acquire them for a song."

"Why come to me?" Zhao had responded. "I have no capacity in the government anymore."

"Ahh, but we know your involvement with the infrastructure attacks in the US. With your expertise, this can be done quite surgically, causing economic pain without the large amount of physical damage that would require extra time and money to repair."

"Let's say I had such power. Why would we do that?" asked Zhao. "We would be hurting ourselves in the reduction of trade."

"It won't be as bad as you think," replied Bludnik. "It will be easy enough to divert your trade to the other ports in the western US. The volume won't change, but the Americans will have to spend more time and money transporting their beloved material goods to their final endpoints."

"I see how it will help you and indirectly help us, but why should we do it instead of you?" asked Zhao.

"Because I will pay you one billion euros for your trouble," replied the European.

When Zhao raised an eyebrow nearly imperceptibly, Bludnik knew he had him.

"This will come in any form you wish. Cryptocurrency would be preferred since it is the easiest to transfer, using multiple coins and trans-actions to keep the authorities at bay. Or we can use cash, precious metals, direct wire transfers, and other means as well—but of course, each method has its limitations."

Zhao knew the limitations well, including his government's ability to track his financial status, so he was already dabbling in cryptocurrency, which could be accessed anywhere in the world. His mind started spinning with options that would open up with such a bankroll.

"This will come to you personally. You can handle it as you see fit. And as a measure of our sincerity," Bludnik said, opening his briefcase, "we give you today approximately one million euros worth of gold and cash—yours to keep whether or not you work with us further."

Bludnik pulled out twenty-five plastic containers holding ten one-ounce gold coins and lined them up on Zhao's desk. He next pulled out an equivalent number of bundles of large-denomination Renminbi and laid them next to the gold.

His mind racing, Zhao asked, "How about another option?"

"I'm open. Let's hear it."

"I would like an island, complete with infrastructure, remote but defensible, transferred to an entity I control anonymously. I'm sure you have an idea where I could get one?"

Bludnik smiled. "I think that could be arranged." They shook hands, even though neither man abided by any degree of being honorable.

"Now," Bludnik said, "how would you go about destroying the trade economy of the Port of Seattle?"

Zhao gave him the first idea that came to his mind that would accomplish the objectives of the European. He then began planning how to get and use the billion euros he was due.

For his part, Bludnik had thought the idea was brilliant and immediately began to scale up the idea mentally. *That was a good use of a billion euros*, he thought.

Shaking his head clear, coming back to the present, Zhao picked up the phone to call this Bludnik fellow.

———

Dr. John Jensen was back in the OR a day after helping with the mob incident. It was his sixth emergency case of the shift, and he was sweating as he worked feverishly to stop the patient's bleeding on the table in front of him. He had gotten shot in a grocery store that was being looted. He didn't know if the guy was a participant in the looting or an innocent bystander. He'd learned long ago it didn't matter to make the distinction because the facts frequently changed over the next few days or weeks anyway.

There, he thought as he tied off the large bleeding artery leading to the small bowel, giving him time to remove the rest of the blood from the abdomen. This also took longer because the hospital was out of suction tubing. He had to use multiple sponges to soak up the blood and pass them off to the scrub tech. Not only did this take longer, but the more sponges he used, the more likely he was to inadvertently leave one inside, a complication that still happened occasionally, despite all the systems employed to prevent it.

He examined the rest of the abdominal cavity looking for additional injuries. He counted six holes in the small bowel, but thankfully, there were no other injuries. The bullet was lodged in the back muscles without active bleeding, so he left it in place. "All right, let's have a stapler," he said to the team.

"Doctor Jensen, we are out of staplers of all sizes," said the circulating nurse.

Jensen took a deep breath and sighed loudly. *This is getting old*, he thought. "Fine, get me some 3-0 silk on an SH needle, then."

The hospital had already run out of all the other more popular sutures, so he was down to using the old standby. "Okay, but this is our last box, so use it wisely," said the veteran nurse.

It always took longer to use sutures than staples, which also increased time under anesthesia, which led to a higher complication rate. The medical staff noticed more complications because of supply chain problems, even though the hospital canceled all elective surgeries. Patients and their families were on edge, taking it out on the hospital staff.

He had to make a decision: either use multiple sutures to resect three segments of the doubly injured bowel or resect the entire large segment of the bowel where they were located and do one anastomosis to connect them back. The problem was that because this segment was so long, the patient would likely have chronic diarrhea for the rest of his life. *If he survives this hospital stay*, he thought.

Jensen chose the latter option, hoping one patient's lifelong discomfort would allow perhaps a few others to survive.

He finished the operation and was relieved the sponge count was correct. Then he went to find the family.

"What do you mean he'll have diarrhea the rest of his life?" demanded his wife.

"I'm sorry, but the damage was too extensive," replied Dr. Jensen. Technically not untrue, but at 3:00 a.m., he was too tired to explain all the details.

He finished with the patient's wife and went back to the ER to see five other surgical patients who had been transferred in from other smaller hospitals that could no longer perform any operations.

"Listen, Doc. We've been waiting for over eighteen hours now with my kid in pain from this appendicitis. Now you're saying it's going to be yet another hour or two? This is ridiculous! Get me another surgeon who can do this right now!"

Jensen bit his tongue, trying hard not to lash back at the man. "I'm sorry, sir, but I'm it. We are all having to work at least twenty-four-hour shifts with all the additional patients from failing surrounding hospitals like yours. Plus, we only have so many surgical teams on duty at any one time. And as I'm sure you can appreciate, we have to take care of those with life-threatening problems first, like the gunshot wound patient I just finished. If your kid had been shot, he would have gone earlier. But thank God he wasn't. Hopefully, things will start to happen a little faster now with the day crew coming on soon."

"It better start going faster! Otherwise, I might have to speed things up myself!" He lifted his shirt to show the doctor his concealed micro-compact pistol.

Jensen got closer to the man so he could speak out of the child's earshot while holding his hands in almost a praying position at waist height. This way, he could instantly disarm or disable the man if necessary. "If you draw that weapon, it will be the last thing you do," whispered Jensen. "You don't know who you're fucking with. Everyone here is doing the best they can with no sleep, no supplies, and no help. You'd best settle down."

The man's pupils dilated as he considered his options. This doctor didn't act like other people he'd threatened in the past. He was different. Not afraid. He softened his look, stepped back, and sat down, putting his head in his hands. "I'm sorry, Doc. It's just that every time he moves or coughs, he's obviously in pain, and I can't fix it."

"I'm sorry too," said Jensen. "It would be nice if the world was back to before the attacks, and we had all we needed. We're doing the best we can," he repeated. "Hopefully, we still have some pain medicine and antibiotics I can give him until his operation. I'll tell the nurse."

Christ, this can't keep going on like this, he thought as he walked out of the room. More surgeons from the now-idled surrounding hospitals could help if they could get through the credentialing bureaucracy, but it was a nightmare in the best of times. Every aspect of a physician's personal and professional life had to be verified by physically checking with the primary sources and accompanied by multiple references of colleagues, a process that usually took months.

Three hours later, he shook his head, rubbed his bloodshot eyes, finished his workup of the ER patients, and logged on to his work email with a cup of lousy coffee next to him. Every day it seemed he got another email "To the Medical Staff" from either Central Supply or the chief pharmacist delineating another unavailable device or drug, and today was no different. Now Foley catheters were in short supply.

So Dr. Jensen was exhausted and irritable when he strode into the office of the CEO, Craig Overstreet, frustrated by the ever-increasing supply shortage that was critical to his work of saving lives.

"First, it was surgical staplers that can't be replaced. Now we're running low on sutures as well?" he fumed at the boyish-looking thirty-seven-year-old.

"What do we do when they run out? Tell the ER patient to grin and bear his ruptured appendix or perforated ulcer or gunshot wound?"

"I'm sorry, John, but my hands are tied. Corporate tells me they are having trouble getting things and are diverting what supplies they get to where they think they're most needed."

"So they're not needed here, is it? We're expendable? What if your wife has a torsed ovary tonight? What if your kid gets hit by a car? Your *whole* job as CEO is to make sure I and my colleagues have enough resources to take care of people! That's it! Do your job!"

"I'm sorry, but Corporate—" said Overstreet.

"Don't give me that corporate bullshit! We all know it's a convenient excuse to blame other people for your failures and avoid accountability!

People are already having needless complications because of this. Now they're going to start dying in greater numbers. I tell you what. From now on, every time I have to tell a patient or family that we can't treat them right, I'm going to give them *your* name and phone number!"

Overstreet started to sweat now.

"Do your job!" said Jensen as he slammed the door on his way out. He forced himself to take slow deep breaths as he made his way to the surgeon's lounge, where his oncoming replacement was waiting.

He was still fuming as he pushed the door open a little too forcefully. The people in the room quit their conversations and stared at him.

He stopped and took another deep breath. They had never seen him like this. "Sorry," he said to no one in particular. *I guess I'm a little worked up right now.*

His partner patted the place at the table next to him. "Have a seat, John. Let me get you some coffee." He did this as much to give him a few more seconds of precious alone time as to give him more caffeine for the drive home. The others went back to their conversations.

Jensen's hands were still clenched when his partner returned. "Thanks, Will."

"Rough night, huh?"

"Rough everything."

"Well, you got their attention." He jerked his head toward the others. "Everyone's been feeling it, but when they see *you* start to lose control, they know it's getting really bad."

"That's because it *is* getting really bad," said Jensen, starting to settle in with his coffee.

Jensen reported on the events of the last twenty-six hours, hoping he didn't forget anything.

"Wow, that *is* bad," said Will when he finished. "Before long, we'll be back to performing Civil War–era medicine."

"That wasn't medicine," said Jensen, looking down at his coffee while shaking his head. "That was sorting the dead from the not-yet dead."

The men sat with their thoughts for a minute more, realizing the enormity of what was to come.

Jensen suddenly felt completely exhausted. With obvious effort, he pushed himself back from the table.

"Go get some sleep," said Will, patting him on the shoulder. "I got this."

"Thanks, see you tomorrow. Call me if you need anything." He knew that if two or more life-threatening emergencies came simultaneously, he would be rushing back, tired or not.

He shuffled his way to his car to head home, nearly nodding off twice into oncoming traffic.

As he walked in from the garage, his wife, Marie, was waiting for him. "I'm glad you're home. We've got a problem."

He took another deep breath and barely raised his eyebrows at her.

"You know the Lewis kids that we let use our basketball hoop, right?"

"Yeah."

"They told me yesterday they are almost out of food. Their mom is giving them just half portions while their dad just sits in front of the TV drinking beer all day."

"Isn't he a lawyer?"

"Yeah, but apparently, not only did neither he nor his wife set *anything* aside for hard times, but they're afraid to go out to any stores with all the looting and riots going on."

"I imagine he's afraid of running into some of his thug clients. Tough problem. Should've thought ahead." He headed back to the bedroom.

"But we need to do something," Marie said to his back. "We can't let them starve!"

"Lemme think about it," he said as he fell into bed, still clothed. "They aren't the only ones, and we can't feed everybody."

———

The technician in Washington monitoring the Chinese contact announced, "Call being made from Zhao's phone. Receiving number is . . ." He checked his monitors. "Receiving number is our target phone in Venezuela. No voice or text message sent."

Inaka allowed himself a small fist pump. "Get that info to the team on the ground. And I hate to say this, but we need to get the attorney general's office in here too. We definitely have international actors working together, and if we're going to bring them to justice, it has to be by the book."

He hoped that the AG's liaison would be a straight-shooter, but these days it could be a partisan hack or even a foreign spy. He had seen other investigations torpedoed for political convenience before.

TWENTY-SIX

"ROGER THAT," SAID ACE, the team leader in Venezuela, after getting the update on the Chinese connection. He then announced, "The target is exiting town to the east into a two-lane road along the coast. The next big town is about thirty miles away. If we hustle, we can get to them before that town. Let's move."

Fifteen minutes later, after careening over rough, winding roads that rattled their kidneys, the teams came in sight of the target vehicle.

"Here's the plan," said Ace. "My car will pass him, and we will get a description of the occupants and contents if possible. We will then execute a descending speed stop. Remember, we need to take this guy alive, but be alert. He's extremely dangerous."

Tom grinned as his body started a little bouncing kind of dance in his rear seat like he always did when he got excited. He had been cooped up too long and needed some action again. Next to him, his Uncle Sam glared at him, and he muted but didn't eliminate his dance.

The cars had slowed from their breakneck pace to match the target car once they sighted it. Now with the plan in place, they accelerated to about five miles an hour over the target speed so they wouldn't spook the driver. When they were in position, the lead car pulled into the opposing lane to pass. Fortunately, the road was empty.

Ace examined the target vehicle as they passed. "We have a military-age Latin male driving, with a similar-age Latin female in the front passenger seat. I see one young child in the back seat—looks to be maybe six or eight. There may be a car seat in there as well. No obvious sign of a European male."

As he watched a car pull out to pass him, Isandro Bautista reflected on the great day he was having with his family. Those seemed rare in Venezuela these days. Everyone was happy from the win on the baseball field, the ice cream afterward, and just spending time together in the sunshine. As the car passed, he noticed five men looking back at him, with one talking.

It completed its pass and pulled back into the right lane but didn't keep the same speed. It gradually slowed to the point where Isandro had to brake. He checked his mirror before pulling out into the opposing lane, only to see another car behind him already doing that. He waited to let that second car pass, but he became alarmed when it stayed even with him. As all three cars continued to decelerate, it clicked in his brain.

"We're being carjacked," he said to his wife.

"No, no, no, no, noooooo!" she cried as she started making signs of the cross repeatedly. "Don't let them take my babies! Don't let them take me! Remember the beauty queen?"

"Yes, I remember. Don't worry."

Everyone in Venezuela knew about the murder of the actress and former Miss Venezuela a few years ago on a road west of Caracas. Carjackers frequently took not just the car but all the valuables and often the women and children as well to rape and sell to human traffickers.

I'm going to live up to my name today, thought Isandro, whose parents had given him the name that meant "liberator" in the expectation that he would liberate his family and perhaps country from the nefarious tyrants. He frantically racked his brain for options. He knew that if they came to a stop, he would be trapped by the car beside him and couldn't defend his family. Just then, a side road appeared toward the tiny village of El Tigrillo. He made a sharp right turn to enter the village, which he knew quite well because a buddy lived there. He was confident he could lose them in its winding streets.

"Shit—target turned right," announced the trailing car as the driver, Cap, skidded to a stop. He reversed back to the turnoff and then spun right to follow him.

The target was already a block ahead and accelerating when Cap's car entered the road. Cap floored it, but that just caused the tires to spin on the dirt road. By the time he regained traction, Ace's car had fallen in behind them. The target was now two blocks ahead as they raced to catch him, knowing that he likely had the information and the codes to disarm the WMDs on the streets of the United States.

What few people were on the village streets instinctively backed off the sidewalks when they heard the three cars tearing through their main street. At what seemed to be the end of the road, the target turned right down another road, still with the two teams behind him. The target ultimately looped back to rejoin the first village road. He fishtailed on the left turn and then again as he turned right back onto the coast road.

"We've got to get this guy," said Ace over the radio. "Whatever it takes."

"Roger that," replied Cap in the new lead car.

Together, all three cars were flying down the coast road, their tires barely remaining on the asphalt as they careened around the sharp turns. Suddenly they saw the target car hit its brakes and spin its tires to the right, but the car did not follow. Instead, it went into the oncoming lane, crossed what little shoulder remained, and then pitched over the side of the cliff and disappeared.

The two team cars barely escaped the same fate, only because they braked a little sooner. They all jumped out, and Tom saw it first.

"Oh, no," he said as he turned away and vomited.

"What is it?" said Ace as he rushed over.

"Oh, shit."

The car was mangled at the bottom of the fifty-foot cliff, upside down, tires still spinning. A small body was lying next to it, with its head at an impossible angle.

"We've got to get down there and look for our target. He may have been on the floor or in the trunk." He pointed at two guys. "You two go to the right down the road to look for a navigable way down. And you," he said, pointing to two others, "go down to the left for the same thing. The rest of us will stay here until the first one says he's there. Then we'll follow. And you two," he pointed to Tom and Sam, "find a place out of sight across the road and let us know if there's trouble coming."

Twenty minutes later, the message from the team near the car came over the radio. "Two here. We are approaching the vehicle now. I see one hanging upside down in the car."

"Copy that," said Ace. "The three of us are coming your way. Four?"

"It's slow-going for us," Dog said. "We'll double back to you."

With guns drawn, team two—Buck and Cap—flanked the car and approached, watching for movement. Cap saw it first, about thirty feet from the vehicle. Eyes open, with blood coming from both ears, the young boy was not breathing, clearly dead.

"One dead child here, continuing to close in."

Tom heard the interchange, and his stomach started to churn again. *This is not an adventure anymore*, he thought.

"One coming in behind you," announced Ace to avoid surprising his teammates, who were now prone on either side of the car.

"I have three dead inside. Two in the front seat—look like husband and wife, and a toddler in the car seat strapped in the back. The man doesn't fit the description of our target."

"Four, keep an eye out for our target on your way down," instructed Ace.

"On it."

Ace reached his teammates as they were getting back up on either side of the car. "We need to get into the trunk." He tried the button, but nothing happened. The two guys got back prone and crawled into the back seat. Cap cut the seat belt holding the car seat with its dead child strapped in place, and it crashed to the roof. He pulled it out, thinking of his toddler at home, and swallowed hard to beat back the rising choking feeling inside.

Buck tried pulling the rear seat back without success and then used his knife to cut into it to get to the flimsy wall of the trunk. It seemed to take forever, but eventually, he accessed the trunk.

"No one here, boss. Just a stroller."

"Shit," said Ace, looking around for another body or movement. "Four, you got anything?"

"Didn't see a thing," said Dog as he came up behind the site.

Ace explained the situation to his control on the trawler. "Are you sure we got the right vehicle?"

"We show the signal from the phone went stationary at your location at the time of the crash. It's there."

"All right," said Ace. "Let's search the adults. Maybe our description is all wrong."

Buck and Cap got back down to cut out the adults and were now overwhelmed by the stench of feces. They fought through it and pulled the people out with the help of Dog and Fletch. Elmer and Ace started going through their clothes while Buck returned to the car to look for a purse.

Elmer found a flip phone on the man. He opened it and found the number for the phone. He handed it to Colonel Flores to look through the contacts and recent numbers to see if they matched what they already had. Buck found another one in the purse and did the same thing.

"I see nothing here that matches the number we saw from the phone in the compound. Nothing looks out of the ordinary."

"Let's tear the car apart," said Ace. "If it's not here, we need to search the path the car took on the way down in case it got ejected. Keep an eye out for another body as well."

Four of the team members dove back into the car. Cap pulled out the stroller to access the trunk. On a hunch, knowing the modular options on strollers better than his teammates, he started pulling it apart.

"Got another phone," he announced.

This was a smart phone and required another passcode to enter it. "We need some more of your magic to get this open," said Ace to the trawler.

"And by the way, this guy obviously hid his phone in this poor family's stroller. We are now back to square one to try to find the guy."

"Someone's coming," said Tom to Sam. A police car came around the corner and then slowed to a stop next to the other two vehicles.

"Trouble," announced Sam to the rest over the radio. "A police officer just pulled up and is getting out of his car."

"Shit," said Ace. "If he radios for help, we're dead. You've got to disable or kill him."

Please don't make me kill a brother officer, thought Sam. There was no way they could cross the street quickly and silently. The man had his back to them, looking over the cliff, and reached for his radio. Sam realized he had no choice, raised his rifle, and shot the man in the upper mid-back, sending him tumbling off the cliff.

Now Sam was the one who felt sick.

TWENTY-SEVEN

SINCE HIS ARRIVAL IN THE MARINA, Demyan made sure to stay in the cabin of his guide's boat. Once they cleared the harbor into the open Caribbean, he decided he was out of any range of land- or ship-based listening devices. He kept his burner phone off for now.

"Take me to Grenada," he said to the guide. "But let's mimic a standard fishing trip on the way there."

"Sí, señor. We may have enough gas to get there."

"Okay, if we need to stop on the way to refuel, that's fine. I just don't want to make a straight line there." He knew the Americans had a way of determining abnormalities in patterns of movement, and he didn't want to trigger any of those processes.

———

Inaka heard the exchanges over his headset. "We had tracked the guy to the marina, right? What was the video feed showing at that time?"

No one answered.

After an awkward pause, the video tech replied, "When I took over my shift, the focus was on the car heading east. I don't know anything about prior to that."

"All right," said Inaka. "This guy bails out of Caracas straight to the marina, ditches his phone after he gets a call, then does what? He has to get on a boat, right? Let's look at all the marine traffic out of that marina from the time he arrived until now. Use all available resources to access security cams, radio traffic, satellite feeds, cell phone records, et cetera."

Ten minutes later, a tech spoke up. "Sir, we may have our target. I examined the video satellite images from the first hour after our guy arrived and correlated them with the transponder signals."

Inaka came over to him as he pointed to his screen. "This vessel here left harbor about thirty minutes after our target arrived there."

"What makes you think it's him?" asked Inaka.

"First, no other boats left the harbor for at least thirty minutes before or after this one. Second . . ." He pushed a button that overlaid boat call sign numbers on all the vessels on the screen. "This is the only boat that doesn't have a call sign attached. Its transponder is off."

"That's gotta be him," said Inaka. "Keep an eye on it and try to figure out where he's going."

"Here's the kicker, sir. He doesn't seem to be in a hurry, at least during the daylight hours we could use for video. He seems to be going around to likely fishing areas, staying for fifteen to twenty minutes, then motoring to the next site, but generally heading east/northeast."

"So it might be just a fisherman who forgot to turn on his transponder," said Inaka. "Nevertheless, we need to get physical eyes on board. Where is he now?"

"Here's the other problem," said the tech. "It's dark there now, and clouds are rolling in."

Inaka groaned and then looked to his liaisons. "Our electronic assets are unavailable now. Who do we have that's closest to this boat's last known location?"

DOD spoke up. "Our comms ship is closest, but they only have electronic guys on board, no operators. The closest operators are still our team on the coast road east of Caracas."

"Any chance the boat could pick up our guys on the coast and return to the target boat? It would be faster than mobilizing and flying a team out of Florida."

"Wow. The risk would be very high because the intelligence gear and knowledge are astronomical."

"Yeah, but the risk of WMDs detonating on American soil is higher."

"I'll bump it up. This is a National Command Authority–level decision."

When Ace and his team finally made it back up the dark trail, Tom and Sam were waiting for them, looking dejected. Ace filled them in on the findings from below while Sam did the same from above.

"We need to get moving. The longer we stay here, the bigger targets we become," said Ace. "We'll take all three of these cars. Buck, you drive Colonel Flores in the police car on lead. No one will suspect foreigners following a police car. Cap, you drive me and the Jensens. Dog, you get the rest. We're going back west to his last known location."

Ace relayed the plan to command. "Negative," was the reply. "We think the target boat is generally headed east—northeast. You are the closest element. There is a marina just east of you in Naiguatá. You are to head there and try to obtain a boat as quietly as possible and head north."

"Roger that," replied Ace, who then turned to the team. "Anyone ever stolen a boat before?"

Once in the cars and underway, Ace turned to the Jensens in the back seat. "This is a shitty business we're in. No way around it. I know it feels like we killed that poor family and that cop. But we were used. We were used by that madman from Caracas who planted that phone. It's an awful feeling, I know. I've had it multiple times. But it doesn't get better by dwelling on it. It only gets better by committing yourself to doing the right thing in the future, righting any wrongs that are before you. Following through on the mission at hand is the most important right now. This guy has the ability to release weapons that may kill or maim thousands or even millions of Americans, maybe even including our own families, who are already suffering from the effects of the Harbor Day attacks. We follow through for them, okay?" He looked them both in the eye.

Tom straightened himself in his seat and took a deep breath. "Yes, sir," he said with renewed determination. Sam was impressed by the transformation and did the same.

Officer Pedro Gonzalez pulled himself back up to the road level just in time to see three sets of taillights fading off to the east. There was no sign of his car. His back was killing him, and his breathing was labored at best. He thanked God he chose to put on his body armor that day. He rolled to his side and keyed his mike.

TWENTY-EIGHT

DEMYAN LAY ON THE BERTH below deck and considered his progress so far. He had caused perhaps irreparable harm to the United States, giving its citizens a small taste of the suffering his family and compatriots back in Hungary had gone through. He had done so through multiple unrelated channels using different aliases, obscuring responsibility for the acts so that no government could focus its resources on finding the plot's originator. He possibly had some close calls where subordinates had failed him, but he was confident his preplanned contingencies were bearing fruit. Plus, the equivalent of five billion euros of assets was safely hidden through cutouts, companies, and trusts on six continents. He was now untraceable on the dark Caribbean Sea, emitting no electronic signals. He let the low, rhythmic rumble of the boat's engines and the gentle rolling of the swells caress him into well-earned sleep.

The comms trawler had been given orders to stay just outside the territorial waters limit but be ready to go to Naiguatá at full throttle if the team was unable to get a boat. They had radar active and could cross-reference all the ships within their range with their corresponding transponder signals. They identified one boat to their northwest that did not have a transponder and assumed it was the same one the NSA satellite had previously identified. It was meandering its way generally eastward.

Leading the three-car convoy, Buck approached the final turn into the marina. Everyone was focused on the destination, but a flicker of movement caught Tom's eye from the side street. It was a man who looked like he was raising a radio to his mouth.

"Hey guys," Tom said. "We have company."

"Four to One." It was Dog on the radio. "We just had a car pull out and block the road behind us."

"Ambush," replied Ace. "Everyone out here, find cover. We're probably going to have to fight our way in."

Ten seconds later, the cars were stopped and empty, with the team members stashed behind trees on either side of the street. Tom went with Ace, since they were on the same side of their car.

"I saw one guy next to that building with a radio," said Tom.

"Good eyes. Thanks." Then Ace turned to the team. "They know we're here. With these trees and buildings, there are plenty of places for them to hide. I don't know how many of them there are. At least two. Plan for more." He consulted his GPS. "The marina is northwest of here, behind the buildings in front of us, across a treed section, then a beach, then the marina. Maybe five hundred yards total. Four, go."

Dog and his two teammates ran from behind Ace and Tom, and the last one patted Ace on the back on his way past. Ace pivoted to point to the rear and raised his rifle. Tom mirrored his actions.

"Good," said Ace. "Do as I do."

Tom's adrenaline was flowing now. He forced his breathing to slow down.

"Four's in place."

"One, moving," said Ace, and he and Tom simultaneously spun around to go past the other two teams to reach the front. They continued this leapfrog maneuver until they were at the tree line leading to the beach. One by one, the teams passed them through the beach to the marina until they were facing backward. They were cleared to move and then spun forward. After just two steps into the sand, they were suddenly chased by incoming fire from somewhere in the trees.

They ran a few more yards before Ace grunted loudly and went down, grabbing his leg. Tom saw what happened, dropped to one knee, and returned fire toward the muzzle flashes. Once they paused, he grabbed the bigger Ace by his shirt collar with one hand and started dragging him backward while continuing to shoot with the other hand.

"Thanks, partner," said Ace, pushing off with his good leg to assist.

He tried to stand up using the injured leg and screamed when it caused a searing pain accompanied by an unnatural bend in his mid-thigh.

They reached the temporary cover at a dry-docked boat and stopped briefly. Ace said to Tom, "Leg's broke. Keep doing what you're doing, and I'll provide cover fire. Use both hands if you need to."

Elmer looked for the closest fast-looking boat with an easy exit out of the marina, jumped aboard, and threw open the engine compartment door. The other teammates provided cover fire from the dock while he found the wires to the starter, cut and stripped the ends, and then touched them together. The engine roared to life, and all but one of the team members clambered aboard.

Moments earlier, Fletch had seen Tom struggling with Ace and ran back to help. With the rest of the team suppressing the fire from the trees, they each draped an arm over their shoulders and half ran to the boat.

Buck had been casting off the lines while the rest of the team returned fire and was holding the last one when they dragged Ace on board.

"Go, go, go!" yelled Buck as he dropped the line and helped get Ace to a supine position on the boat floor.

Elmer slammed the throttle forward and nearly dumped Tom and Fletch off the back into the water. Since they were already down, they pointed their rifles off the back to suppress fire from that direction.

They cleared the jetty protecting the marina, and the incoming fire stopped.

Tom turned his attention to Ace, whose eyes were closed. "His thigh bone is broken," Tom said to Fletch. "We need to splint it." He looked around his immediate area. "Give me that long seat-back cushion and that line."

Fletch looked where he was pointing and immediately understood. He handed Tom the items and positioned himself at Ace's feet. "This is gonna hurt for a minute," Fletch said as he grabbed Ace's foot and leaned back a little to keep it straight.

Tom positioned the cushion longwise under Ace's leg and then folded it along either side until the edges met at the top. He then secured it by wrapping the line around it.

"I'm impressed," said Fletch. "Where'd you learn that?"

"I took a wilderness first aid course once. Never thought I'd have to use it."

They were racing at top speed to the north. With every swell they crossed, Ace would groan a little, but his eyes remained closed.

Fletch told the team, "He's losing blood. He needs a hospital. What's the plan, Two?"

The team automatically understood that Buck was now in operational control of the team. Then the voice from the trawler came over the radio. "Maintain heading for about ten miles. We will meet you. We are arranging medical ex-fil."

"Roger that," replied Buck. Then to the team, "After we transfer him to that boat, we are going after the bad guy. I just hope they have a bead on him by now."

———

"Copy that, launching now," said the deck watch officer into the radio. The USCG *Boulder*, out of Charleston, South Carolina, was on duty in the central-eastern Caribbean, ready to provide support to any US assets within its large operational range. The Charleston base command had just ordered them to execute a nighttime rescue mission for an American on board a boat off the coast of Venezuela to help the man in critical condition with a broken leg.

The 418-foot *Boulder* had for this deployment an MH–60 helicopter that was crewed by two pilots, a machine gunner–mechanic, and a rescue swimmer. The flight distance was 240 miles, well within the round-trip range for the chopper.

Once the helicopter was launched, the deck watch officer announced, "Change heading to 180, increase speed to twenty-eight knots. Notify Medical that we have a critical patient inbound." She wanted to minimize the time to definitive care for this patient.

———

Elmer reached the ten-mile mark and slowed his engine. "We're at ten miles now, advise."

"We've got you," came the trawler. "Flashing our lights now."

Elmer saw the lights to the north, maybe half a mile away. He needed the lights since any available light from the moon or stars was obscured by the cloud cover. "Heading your way. Our patient is unresponsive now." He accelerated in that direction. Above the boat on the horizon, Elmer he could see what looked like aircraft lights. "That ought to be the rescue chopper. Shouldn't be long now."

When Elmer reached the comms boat, its commander came to the side of his boat to talk with Buck. "We've got the guy painted with radar. He hasn't changed his pattern since we started, so I don't think he's onto us. We'll vector you in from back here. The rescue chopper is on its way for your guy. We'll get him to it ASAP."

"Copy that."

Once Ace had been transferred, the commander ordered, "Assume heading of 275, distance approximately fifteen miles."

TWENTY-NINE

HAVING RETURNED TO THEIR STOLEN BOAT, the rest of the team was focused on the threat at hand. They were lost briefly in their thoughts about Ace and, one by one, realized he was out of their control and would get the best medical care available.

The mission now was to capture the man responsible for the mayhem the planet was now engulfed in. He was out there on the pitch-black sea, trying to be invisible.

Yet the US team was effectively blind in the complete darkness, with no guidance systems on board, having to trust the trawler was giving them correct information. Occasionally the comms ship would give them course corrections. They were not using running lights, so hopefully, they would stay hidden from the target vessel until the last minute. They did not see the faint bursts of lightning on the horizon behind them.

Then they got the news they'd been waiting to hear.

"Be advised," the trawler commander said, "target is about one mile ahead of you to the northwest, heading at 060 degrees, twelve knots."

"Copy that," said Buck, who then gave instructions to Elmer. "Slow to half speed to keep our noise down. We'll circle behind him, then slowly come up on his left flank, standard marine interdiction."

"Roger," replied Elmer, who backed off the throttle.

The swells were getting bigger now with the approaching storm. They could start to see whitecaps cresting them nearby. It would make any boat-to-boat interaction trickier and more dangerous.

———

The fishing boat's captain was focused ahead and kept one eye on the lightning to his right while gradually increasing his speed to outrun the approaching storm. The sudden appearance of bright lights to his left, accompanied by loud thumps and yelling voices, scared him half to death. Speechless, he instinctively pulled back the throttle, took his hands off the steering wheel, and raised them.

The boat was pushed to the right by the next swell and then was struck broadside by the bigger one behind it, pitching Dog off the starboard side into the black water. Tom, still on the first boat with Elmer, was the only one to see Dog hit his head on a pole and fall limply into the water. He threw an available life ring in after him, hit Elmer on the shoulder and pointed, and then jumped off the gunwale into the churning water.

As the yelling in a foreign language got louder, the fishing boat captain raised his hands higher. A couple of the men who had jumped on board the smaller vessel rushed below deck and then returned after several seconds, shaking their heads at the leader. Finally, a Venezuelan military officer stepped forward, addressing the captain in Spanish, "Where is the other man?"

"I don't know what you're talking about!"

"You left the harbor with a man on board. Did you drop him off somewhere? Transfer him to another boat?"

"No, I swear! I am alone! I've always been alone! If someone is here, he snuck aboard, but I don't know where he could hide without my knowledge. I will show you all the spaces big enough for a man, and you can see for yourself."

"Fine, do it."

Meanwhile, Tom was struggling in the high swells in the dark. Although he was a good swimmer, he had never encountered seas this harsh and they were getting the best of him. The water was rough and cold. He headed toward the life ring, grabbed it, and then saw a flash of a body about ten yards beyond, face down. He swam as fast as he could, and once he reached Dog, he turned his body face up. He then placed the life ring over his chest and sequentially brought each arm through to lay over the ring. Another swell hit them when his mouth was open, causing Tom to inhale seawater.

Tom lost his grip on Dog. He went under for a few seconds and came up sputtering. He looked around. *Where is he?* He saw him on the back side of the next swell. He was getting more fatigued by the second. He swam behind Dog and grabbed his collar to pull his head up onto the ring. He then used the attached line to drape over Dog's wrists. When he pulled the line taught behind his head, the lines secured Dog's arms over the ring.

Elmer had broken off, focusing his flashlight on where Tom had pointed. Finally, he saw the white ring and headed the boat slowly toward it. The last thing he wanted was to run over his teammates.

Tom had one arm hooked over the ring's line and was towing Dog back toward the lights with one arm and his feet. His waterlogged clothes and shoes added to the weight, pulling him under. He was working so hard and breathing so hard that he inhaled more and more seawater.

He was out of breath. His vision narrowed as his strokes became weaker. Another wave hit, this time holding him under longer. He felt his arm holding the ring line loosen, and the line slid over his wrist. His fingers clenched but grabbed only water. It was eerily quiet.

He felt himself sinking, breathless, but finally calm. Then he was jerked upward hard by his collar, with his shirt almost choking him. Bright lights shone in his face as he coughed/vomited seawater onto whoever was next to him. He followed the soiled pantleg up to see Sam at the other end, his hand still on his collar. He was on a boat and saw Dog supine beyond him, also coughing. His head dropped back with a thud.

"We've got no joy on this boat. His transponder has been broken for a month, and he says he came from a different harbor. Do you have any other ideas?" said Buck to the trawler.

"Negative." And then, a long second later, the trawler said, "Wait, one."

After another minute, the trawler announced, "You're not going to believe this, but a small boat just exited the radar shadow of a freighter that's hugging the coast about a mile offshore. It also has no transponder signal, and it's heading toward Naiguatá."

"Fuck!" shouted Buck as he slammed his fist onto the dash. The lightning was getting closer, and the wind was picking up.

"Now we have to go back? *Into* the storm?" he shouted incredulously.

"We see no other targets that fit the profile at this time. Godspeed," said the trawler commander.

They were all back on the faster boat now. Elmer swung the bow to their new heading and opened the throttle to its peg.

———

Demyan was jarred awake by the rougher swells now. He shook his head to clear the cobwebs and then swung his feet off the berth onto the deck. After a few more seconds, he stood up and headed toward the bridge.

"Soon after you went below, a storm started forming on the horizon. I stayed leeward behind the freighter to keep it smoother for you, but we need to go to a harbor right now."

That's ironic, thought Demyan. "Very well. Where is it?" He eyed the lightning approaching.

"About half an hour from here. It's called Naiguatá."

The name meant nothing to him. He started making plans. He needed to keep moving. "Tell me about it."

THIRTY

THE US TEAM RACED BACK to shore. The spray from the bow was so fierce that it stung their faces, forcing them to crouch behind cover, except Elmer, who just took it head-on. It was starting to rain also.

With the noise of the engines drowning out other noise, Sam was sitting on the deck with his arm protectively around Tom. "You scared me!" he shouted into Tom's ear.

Tom leaned forward to cough and retch some more. Then he responded, "You should've been on my end!"

"What were you thinking?"

"Everyone else was busy! He needed help!"

"Got it! How're you feeling?" Sam shouted.

"Well, you know Dad always says, 'Get comfortable being uncomfortable.' I guess I'm comfortable now."

The trawler radioed, "Be advised, based on your current heading and speed, you will get to the harbor about one to two minutes after the target boat."

"Yeah, I've been thinking about that," replied Buck. "They were shooting at us when we left. Somehow they knew about us. It's going to be a hornet's nest going back. I'm open to other ideas."

The rain fell harder—the wind picked up more, and the swells were higher, which dropped the boat harder into the troughs. The men were completely drenched. Each slam added bruises on top of bruises. Yet no one cared.

"Just around the point to the east is a fairly wide beach," said the trawler. "That looks like your best option to disembark."

He makes it sound like a cruise, thought Buck, who briefly considered cussing him out. Instead, he answered, "Roger that, diverting now." He pointed Elmer to the left about five degrees.

———

Demyan was next to the skipper on the bridge, watching the lights of the approaching harbor in between lightning bursts. It seemed busier than a typical harbor, with a lot of flashing emergency lights. He was glad he was on a covered bridge rather than enduring the sideways blowing rain.

As Demyan's fishing boat ducked behind the protective jetty, the waters calmed noticeably. They found an open slip to maneuver into. Once they were in place and Demyan jumped off to throw mooring lines back, the two of them were swarmed by at least a dozen armed men in uniform, yelling and gesturing them to the ground.

This is a good sign, Demyan thought.

"Thanks for meeting me," he said to the leader of the swarm. "Your commander, Patricio Navarro, is a good friend of mine. I'm sure he called to have you bring me a car?"

The leader looked confused.

"Do you want me to call him for you? I'd be happy to, but you know how he gets when he's interrupted in the middle of the night if you know what I mean."

Everyone in the Polícia Nacional knew the commander's proclivities. The last officer to violate his orders took a small jump off a tall bridge.

Demyan surveyed the heavily armed police presence. "Surely this is not all for me, is it?"

Then, leveraging his command presence on top of the police sergeant's confusion, he shouted to be heard over the driving rain, "What happened here?"

The sergeant gave him the details, ending with, "They escaped in a boat fleeing north. We were shooting but don't know if we hit any of them."

"And your man said they spoke English?"

"Yes, sir."

Demyan motioned for the sergeant to follow him as he hurried to the shelter of the office building overlooking the marina.

It has to be the Americans, he thought. *I'm surprised they are this close. But at least they're heading away from me now.*

"I still need a car, sergeant."

"You can take mine. Please remember me when you next see Commander Navarro."

"Of course. Thank you." He gripped the man's shoulder to affect compassion when he really felt utter contempt for him. *These people are all alike.*

Buck's boat still had no running lights, so even though they could see all the emergency vehicles at the harbor, no one could see or even hear them in the storm. They rounded the point to the east and looked for the beach.

"There," pointed Buck to a sliver of lighter color. Elmer headed in. Once they grounded out on the beach, they all jumped off, with Tom grabbing a bow line on the way. He tied it to a tree next to the rest of the group.

The rain was coming down even harder now as Buck announced, "There is a road just inland. We'll get to it and follow it west to the marina, then reassess."

The lightning and thunderbolts were striking more frequently and closer by the minute. As they rounded the corner along the muddy road, they were startled by a simultaneous flash and a boom. A few seconds later, there was a loud crack as if a rifle had been fired. They looked toward the source just in time to witness a huge tree fall across the road just feet in front of them. If they had hit the beach twenty seconds earlier, they would all be dead now.

Over the tree now in front of them, they could see the lights of the marina. Buck turned to the group. "We need to do a stealthy insertion into a hostile environment to extract one man that won't want to come with us. Sam, Tom, and Colonel Flores, since you haven't trained with us for years to do this, you will stay here. We'll let you know when we are on our way back with him."

The three nodded affirmatively, and the other five jumped the tree to head to the marina. Within seconds they were no longer visible.

The team spread out to advance on the marina, identified by the lights through the trees. Normally, the police would search every inch of the surrounding area for evidence leading to any suspects, but out of sight of their commander, they were not keen on enduring the pelting rain in the dark woods. So one policeman stood at the edge of the woods with two more under an awning with their suppressed rifles. Buck said into his radio, "I got front guy."

Dog replied, "I got left."

Fletch answered, "I got right."

"Three, two, one," Buck announced, and three simultaneous suppressed rifle shots struck the heads of the three policemen, dropping them instantly without a sound.

As the US team made their way around the last building, they saw a police car heading toward the road leading to their teammates. In the crack of a lightning strike, they caught the face of the driver: a European male.

Buck risked a look around the corner of the main building at the marina toward the group of officers and flashing lights. Because he didn't see any other male who looked European, he had to assume the man in the cop car was their target.

He quickly motioned to his guys to retreat, and they all started running back to their downed tree.

"Okay, guys, he's driving a police car headed your way. Don't kill him, but don't let him get away either," Buck radioed to Sam.

"Roger that," replied Sam, who then conferred with Tom and Flores. "He's coming this way. Spread out, but stay behind the tree. He'll stop. Then you pop up and shoot out his engine block. He can't go anywhere after that."

Flores and Tom went to either side of Sam for about twenty feet and crouched. They saw the headlights come toward them and then stop. All three simultaneously stood up and fired multiple rounds into the car's engine.

Demyan jumped out of the car and ran into the jungle.

Tom was closest to him and jumped the tree to follow him. The rain and darkness obscured most of his vision, but the lightning strikes illuminated movement periodically. Tom thrashed through the jungle, single-mindedly focused on the prey in front of him.

Demyan hesitated for a second at a junction, trying to decide which path to take, when Tom leaped at him. Just then, Demyan lurched to the right, leaving only his feet within Tom's reach. But Tom grasped one foot and held on for dear life, face down in the mud.

Demyan writhed and struggled to get away for what seemed like minutes when suddenly Tom heard a crash to his left accompanied by bright lights in his face. A figure rushed in front of him. He heard a thud and realized that Demyan was no longer thrashing about.

Tom felt a hand on his shoulder.

"You okay?" It was Cap. "Good catch." Tom looked the other way to see Fletch putting zip ties on Demyan's wrists behind his back.

Buck compared his face to the sketch on his phone and then announced through the radio, "It's him. Everyone, back to the beach where we inserted. We need to get out once the storm weakens."

They half ran, half-dragged Demyan back to the beach and the tree holding their boat.

"Tell us where the WMDs are," commanded Buck.

Demyan looked up and realized that was their objective. He would try to leverage it against them.

Buck added, "You're going to prison for a very long time."

"No, I'm not."

"You sound so sure of yourself. Why not?"

"You think I arranged all this? I'm nobody. You probably don't even know my real name."

Buck started to get a chill up his spine.

"Go on."

"I work for a small group of people. A group that owns and controls the levers of power across the globe. People that are so rich you've never heard of them. If you work with me, I'll give you their names. If you don't, they will get me out anyway. Either way, I'm a free man. You can either have something to show for it . . . or nothing."

Buck stared at him for a moment and then growled, "Get him to the boat. We need to beat feet before anyone comes looking for him."

The tide had come in, and the boat was now floating, fortunately still tied to the tree. Cap pulled it in as far as possible to the beach and waved his arm to signal the others to get on board. He then undid the line from the tree and ran back with it to jump on himself. Elmer had gotten the boat started again and expertly spun it around to head back out toward the storm, which was moving north.

Buck got on the radio, "Control, we have our suspect in good condition. We are feet wet heading north. Advise where you want us to take him." He looked at the fuel gauge. "We are getting low on fuel."

"Roger that," replied the trawler. "Head northwest at 330 degrees. The storm is moving north over us now. You can slow down as needed to keep on the back side of it. We will meet you to offload everyone."

"Copy that, thanks," Buck replied. He was tired and ready to get to friendly territory.

———

Four hours later the team and their suspect finally arrived at the trawler. After transferring the other eight men to the now very crowded communications ship, Elmer removed the drain plugs at the back of the stolen boat to sink it to eliminate any evidence the Americans may have left on board.

The helmsman then wheeled the ship northward as the commander addressed the new arrivals. "We have another chopper coming to pick up your suspect. They only have room for six people—total. You decide who else is going."

In a welcome change, it was a bright morning with calm seas as the helicopter grew from a speck in the sky approaching their vessel. The telltale "whump-whump" of the rotor noise grew louder, and Buck said to the men, "Dog, you and Fletch will be security for our detainee, so you go first, then the suspect. Colonel Flores next, then our two guests, the Jensens." Buck turned to them and said, "Gentlemen, you proved yourselves to be valuable members of this team. We couldn't have accomplished this mission without you." He then looked Tom in the eye and said, "You, young man, saved our butts more than once. I wish you all the best for the rest of your life. You can do anything you put your mind to. And I speak for our whole team when I say that we would be honored to go into battle with you again."

Tom's eyes teared up, and a lump formed in his throat as he reached to take Buck's offered hand. "Thank you very much," Tom croaked.

The helicopter's noise prevented further talking, and one by one, the passengers were hoisted up. Once all were aboard and strapped in, the crewman said, "You guys have been busy."

Tom asked, "Did you pick up Ace?"

"We did."

"Where'd you take him?"

"We stopped at the ship to refuel and get him some blood, then took him to the Trauma Center in Puerto Rico. He was in bad shape."

"How's he doing now?" Tom asked.

"Don't know. We've been busy too," the crewman replied.

"Is that where we're going?"

"Kind of. We need to stop at the ship to refuel. Then we're taking you all to the Coast Guard Air Station at Aguadillo, Puerto Rico. They have law enforcement facilities there to hold the detainee for now."

———

Upon landing at the Coast Guard Air Station, the commander led a small team to approach the disembarking passengers. "We have a secure room for the suspect." He pointed to one of his men as Dog and Fletch each took one of Demyan's arms to follow.

"Colonel Flores?"

"Yes, sir."

"We have a team waiting for you." He pointed to another officer, who motioned for Flores to follow.

The commander looked at a small notecard. "Sam Jensen?"

"Yessir."

"Director Burroughs is sending a jet down here in a few hours to get the suspect to Washington. He wants you and Tom to be on that plane."

Sam replied, "Yes, sir."

Tom asked, "Where's Ace? His teammates and I want to see him."

The commander thought for a moment. "You have earned that right to see him. The trauma center is a chopper ride away from here in San Juan. I'll arrange one for you once the prisoner is secured. You can be back here in time to catch that plane north."

"Thank you very much, sir."

———

An hour later, Tom, Sam, Dog, and Fletch walked into Ace's room in the Trauma Intensive Care Unit. Ace was lying in bed, eyes closed, intubated with a breathing tube in his mouth. Tom saw the ventilator pumping air through the clear plastic circuit tubing into his lungs. A nasogastric tube was draining stomach fluid from his nose into a canister on the wall. A bag containing urine was hanging on the bed rail, peeking out below the sheet covering him. IV lines snaked out from under the sheet connected to pumps mounted on poles by the bed. Two monitors above the head of the bed had different colors of squiggly lines, all moving continuously. Multiple different beeping noises combined with the sound of the ventilator made it anything but quiet.

The team felt another person enter the room behind them, who moved to the foot of the bed. "Hi, I'm Doctor Sanchez. Who are you guys?"

"We are part of the team that was with Ace when he got injured," Dog replied.

Doctor Sanchez tilted his head forward in respect and paused for a deep breath. "Technically, I'm only supposed to talk to family about him, but I'm former military, so I know you *are* his family.

"I was here when the Coast Guard brought him in. He was in shock; his thigh was blown up like a balloon. The medics told me you guys had to pull him out of the firefight and then fashioned a makeshift splint on the speeding boat. They were very impressed."

The team just looked at him.

"You guys saved his life long enough to get him here. He wouldn't be here without you. His main artery and vein to the leg were both injured by the bullet, as was the femur itself. We have placed temporary shunts to move the blood flow around the injured segments of bone and have temporarily fixated the bone to keep it stable to prevent more injury." He pulled back the sheet over Ace's leg to show a cage-like contraption with long pins going through the skin like spokes on a wheel at the upper and lower thigh.

"This is called an external fixator. The pins are drilled into the bone to keep it all stable. Hopefully, in a day or two, he will be stable enough for us to go back to the operating room to fix his vascular injuries definitively. But he will likely need to be in the hospital for a few weeks at best, with more operations needed."

Tom looked at Ace lying helpless in that bed, his mind churning through the events of the past week and contemplating his future. He reached under the sheet for Ace's hand and gripped it in an improvised handshake. He was surprised by a barely perceptible grip back in return.

Please help him, God. He needs more time to help right the wrongs in this world, Tom thought, with another lump forming in his throat.

Fletch spoke up, "What can we do for him now, Doc?"

"Just pray for him," Sanchez replied. "We're supporting him until his body can take over the healing process. It will happen in the next twenty-four to forty-eight hours, or it won't."

The team turned toward Ace, lost in their thoughts and prayers. At last, one of the helmeted helicopter crewmen entered to say, "Gentlemen, the commander says it's time to go."

"Copy that," Dog said. "Let's go, guys."

Tom released his grip, took a deep breath, dried his eyes, and followed the others out of the room.

———

The helicopter carrying the four men touched down at the Coast Guard Air Station to find an unmarked Gulfstream V jet parked in front of the hangar next to the control tower. As they disembarked the helicopter, they saw Demyan being escorted out of the hangar, shackled between two beefy US marshals. They all ascended the jet, assumed the closest open seat, and promptly succumbed to the fatigue earned over the last few days.

They were awakened by the touchdown of the landing gear at Ronald Reagan Washington National Airport. They smacked their lips and shook their heads to clear them.

Two black SUVs pulled up to the aircraft as the cabin door opened. Demyan and the marshals entered the first one while the Jensens entered the other. Together, the vehicles made the ten-minute drive from the airport to the FBI Headquarters on Pennsylvania Avenue, where they both entered the open ramp going to the basement parking lot of the building. An attendant closed the open gate behind them.

The vehicles pulled up to a bank of two elevators and stopped beside two agents with earpieces, who moved to the rear doors. The agent in front opened the door first, pointed to the elevator on the right, and watched the marshals escort their prisoner inside before following.

The second then opened Sam's door. "Are you the Jensens?"

"Yes," Sam replied.

"Follow me," said the agent as he climbed into the left elevator.

"Where are we going?" asked Tom.

"The director's office. Top floor," came the reply.

The elevators opened to a room with another agent at a desk, who stood to open the door to the next room. A receptionist there oversaw a few chairs with one man present they didn't recognize. She stood and said, "The director is ready to see you all."

She led them into the spacious office, and Deputy Director Burroughs stood from behind his desk, walked around it to shake all their hands, and led them to the small conference table nearby.

"I am glad to finally meet you guys. I don't think you know each other, but Chuck Haggard, I want you to meet Sam and Tom Jensen." They all shook hands.

Burroughs continued, "Chuck is with the New York Police Department Human Trafficking Unit, and he was instrumental in finding and apprehending the main suspect in the Port of New York/New Jersey attacks. He just flew in from Austin with his suspect yesterday. Superb work."

Tom raised his eyebrows. "Austin? Interesting. My folks live there."

Haggard remembered Dr. Jensen telling him his son and brother were involved in South America. "I know. I met your father. Very impressive man. Looks like it's a family trait."

"Gentlemen, we will do your formal debriefings after this. But I already know enough to know that the United States of America needs you to continue your great work to bring the rest of these evil people to justice. I would like for you three to form the nucleus of a new group I'm forming for this mission. I will make sure you have all the resources you need to accomplish it."

Tom's jaw dropped. Sam and Haggard were more composed but just as surprised.

Haggard spoke first, "I would be honored, sir."

Sam was next, "Same here, sir."

Tom thought about Ace lying helpless in his ICU bed in Puerto Rico and answered, in a surprisingly calm manner, "Yes, sir, I'll do whatever it takes."

"Thank you very much," Burroughs replied. "The country already appreciates your excellent work and your sacrifice. We took the liberty of getting toiletries and clothes for you guys, as well as hotel rooms. Take a couple of hours to get cleaned up before we start the formal debriefing."

The three men stood and walked out to the open office, where they found three piles of clothes and already-bagged toiletries. Haggard and Sam headed to the outer door when Tom asked the assistant, "Can I use your phone?"

"Of course," she replied. "Do you need a number?"

"No, ma'am, thank you."

———

John Jensen looked at his phone to see a call from a number he didn't recognize. "Hello, it's Dr. Jensen."

"Hey, Dad."

"Wow, it is great to hear your voice, son! I've been worried sick. Where are you?"

"I'm in Washington, DC, believe it or not, with Uncle Sam, and we're fine. We've got a lot going on still, but I wanted to give you a call."

"I'm glad you did. Your mother will be delighted to hear you're safe."

"Tell her not to worry. We're good. But you'll be happy to hear this. You know how you've been harping at me ever since college about how I need to get a real career?"

"Of course."

"Well, I know what I want to do with my life."

ABOUT THE AUTHOR

MARK DICKSON is a retired surgeon and combatives enthusiast who, after successfully raising four children, moved with his wife to a farm in rural Texas, where they enjoy caring for the land and rescuing animals.

Made in the USA
Coppell, TX
18 October 2023

22995421R00132